They were the only survivors of the crash.

That meant they were completely alone and in the wilderness. Aside from the dangers of exposure, there were wild animals to contend with.

Eva's gut clenched around a hard knot of fear. "What the hell is going on? And where is Decker Newcombe if he got thrown off the stretcher?"

"I don't think he got thrown off at all." With the toe of his boot, Brett nudged the railing. "That handcuff has been unlocked."

He was right. There was another handcuff that lay next to the first. It was unlocked, as well. She knelt and stared at the US marshal's dead body before them. There was bruising on his neck, and his windpipe had collapsed.

"His throat has been crushed," she said. "He didn't just die of his wounds. He was killed."

Then she understood everything. Somehow, Decker had gotten out of the stretcher, taken the marshal's keys and then killed the man.

She and Brett weren't just stranded and alone. They were lost, and a serial killer was on the loose.

And if they weren't careful, they might just become his next victims.

Dear Reader,

Welcome back to Texas Law. I'm thrilled to continue this series with the same amount of excitement, danger and desire—but with a new cast of characters. In fact, the things I love most about *Stranded* are the hero and heroine.

Brett Wilson is a medevac pilot and forever the optimist. Eva Tamke, a nurse, has a lot going on in her life and isn't looking for a new relationship. But the duo is set up on a date. The chemistry is real, and a nice dinner turns into a night of passion. Because of a family emergency, Eva only has time for their single night. After he gets the news from Eva that their budding relationship is being pruned from the vine, even Brett's sunny disposition can't keep him from feeling disappointed.

When Eva shows up to fill in as the nurse on his flight crew, things are awkward. But after their helicopter crashes in the Texas desert, they have to rely on each other to survive the elements and escape from an at-large serial killer.

The attraction from before can't be ignored, and both Eva and Brett realize that they're better together than apart. Will it be enough to keep them alive while they're *stranded*?

Read and find out!

All the best,

Jennifer D. Bokal

STRANDED

JENNIFER D. BOKAL

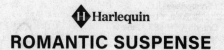

ROMANTIC SUSPENSE

Harlequin®
ROMANTIC SUSPENSE™

Recycling programs for this product may not exist in your area.

ISBN-13: 978-1-335-50263-6

Stranded

Copyright © 2024 by Jennifer D. Bokal

Harlequin Enterprises ULC
22 Adelaide St. West, 41st Floor
Toronto, Ontario M5H 4E3, Canada
www.Harlequin.com

Printed in Lithuania

MIX
Paper | Supporting responsible forestry
FSC® C021394

Jennifer D. Bokal is the author of several books, including the Harlequin Romantic Suspense series Rocky Mountain Justice, Wyoming Nights, Texas Law and several books that are part of the Colton continuity.

Happily married to her own alpha male for more than twenty-five years, she enjoys writing stories that explore the wonders of love. Jen and her manly husband have three beautiful grown daughters, two very spoiled dogs and a cat who runs the house.

Books by Jennifer D. Bokal

Harlequin Romantic Suspense

Texas Law

Texas Law: Undercover Justice
Texas Law: Serial Manhunt
Texas Law: Lethal Encounter
Stranded

The Coltons of Owl Creek

Colton Undercover

The Coltons of New York

Colton's Deadly Affair

The Coltons of Colorado

Colton's Rogue Investigation

Visit the Author Profile page
at Harlequin.com for more titles.

To John
On this journey of life, I'm glad that you're by my side.

Chapter 1

The scent of salsa, fried corn chips and cinnamon hung in the air. Eva Tamke wiped her mouth with a paper napkin and set it onto the empty plate. Warmth crept up her chest and settled onto her cheeks. The heat had nothing to do with the spicy food she'd eaten or the margarita she'd finished an hour earlier.

It was all because of the man who sat across the table.

Brett Wilson was a medevac pilot at San Antonio Medical Center—the same place she worked as an ER nurse. The medical center was so large that she'd never met him before tonight.

After months of being matched only with creeps on dating apps, Eva was beyond dubious when a mutual friend from work promised that Brett was perfect. But he was. Heck, they even shared a history of serving in the armed forces. He'd been full-time army, flying Black Hawks, and had served overseas more than once. She'd been in the Air Force Reserve, using the GI Bill to pay for college.

Thank goodness she'd worn her favorite dress—a coral sundress with spaghetti straps and tight bodice that fell to her knees. The color matched her lipstick perfectly and brought out the caramel highlights in her brown hair. Truly, in this dress, she felt confident. Even beautiful.

And for the first time in what seemed like forever, she wanted to be attractive for a man—this man. Brett was tall, over six feet if she had to guess. He had broad shoulders, blond hair, blue eyes and a square jaw. His jeans hugged his rear and the cuff of his blue T-shirt accentuated the muscles in his biceps.

"So, what do you think?" he asked, pointing to her plate. "Was I right? Or was I right? That was the best burrito in all of San Antonio."

"It was good," she said, being honest. The chicken had been fresh and tender. The cheese was mellow. The beans had a spicy kick. "Then again, you only have food from an army base for comparison," she said, bringing up the old joke that army fare was horrible, while the air force fed their people well. In all honesty, she didn't know if the joke was true or not. She'd never eaten at an army facility. They'd talked about their military service, swapping stories, and he'd felt like someone she'd known for years. Comfortable. Familiar. And excitingly brand-new at the same time. "There's a Tex-Mex restaurant near my apartment. The food there is excellent, too."

"Excellent is nice," he said, smiling. In the dark restaurant, his teeth were brilliantly white. "But this was perfection."

"Perfection is pretty hard to come by." With Brett, she liked being flirty and charming. She flipped her hair over her shoulder.

Brett reached across the table and traced the back of her hand. An electric current danced along her skin.

"Trust me." Again, he gave her that smile. Her cheeks warmed even more. "I know perfection when I see it."

She let him slip his fingertips between her own. Her pulse spiked. For a moment, she almost forgot about the call she'd gotten earlier in the day.

Her sister. Katya told her that their grandmother had fallen. Baba was taken to the hospital near Eva's childhood hometown of Encantador, Texas. Thankfully, Baba had only sprained her ankle. But the doctor had been clear: their grandmother could no longer live alone.

It brought up an interesting predicament. Katya shared a three-bedroom house with her husband and three kids. The home, though filled with love, was already too crowded to add an elderly lady who needed care.

Eva lived in San Antonio and worked full-time.

Their father and his new wife had moved to California almost two decades earlier.

Aside from the three of them, there was no other family.

Her grandmother had always resisted moving into an assisted living community. Eva had to do something...

Her mind drifted back to the restaurant. Nearby, a server placed an upside-down chair on a table. Another server pushed a broom across the floor.

She inclined her head toward the workers. "Looks like they want us to get out of here."

She could easily spend another hour here, talking, sharing, getting to know him. They'd covered all the first-date topics—basics about their families and where they were from, favorite foods and movies. They had a

lot in common. They'd both even served in the military
years before. Between their easy back-and-forth and her
attraction to him, she'd managed not to let her sister's
call trouble her during the date.

"I guess so." Still holding her hand, Brett rose from
the table. She stood as well. "I'll walk you to your car."

He led her through the empty restaurant and pushed
the door open. It didn't matter that the sun had set hours
earlier, it was still hot outside. Sweat collected at the
nape of her neck and pooled at the small of her back.

"Where's your car?" he asked.

The restaurant sat in the middle of a shopping plaza
adjacent to a sprawling neighborhood. At this time of
night, the parking lot was all but empty. Her car, a dark
blue sedan, was two rows back, bathed in the glow of
a tall lamppost.

"It's over there," she said.

"I'll walk with you."

With her hand in his, they crossed the parking lot.
Using a fob to start the engine, she unlocked the doors.
The date, it seemed, was over. But she really didn't want
the night to end.

"So," Brett said, stepping toward her.

"So," she echoed, closing the distance between them.

Brett leaned toward her, touching his lips to hers. A
spark ran through her body, and despite the heat, she
wanted him closer. Wrapping her arms around his neck,
she ran her fingers over the nape of his neck and pulled
him close.

He gave a low growl. She felt the sound in her middle.
It traveled to her toes and left her knees weak. Sighing,

she stepped back. "Thanks for taking me out. It's been a long time since I've had this much fun on a date."

"It doesn't have to end," said Brett. "We can go to my house for a drink." He pointed to the neighborhood next to the shopping center. "I live over there."

"I really shouldn't have any more alcohol. The margarita's out of my system, but…"

"Coffee, then," he said, before adding, "I even have decaf if you prefer. So it won't keep you up all might."

It was too hot for coffee. But she didn't care. Brett was more than handsome and funny. Talking to him was like getting together with an old friend, rather than meeting someone new. Then again, she didn't usually go home with men on the first date. At thirty-six years of age, she'd gained some wisdom. She knew that one-night stands were just that—a distraction for one night.

With Brett, she saw the potential for more.

But her life wasn't so simple. Her grandmother's accident had made things complicated, and she had some tough choices to make.

Brett's lips were oh, so kissable. His arms were strong, and his legs were long. Just standing next to him left her toes tingling. Maybe what she needed was a distraction for one night. And she found herself saying, "A decaf coffee would be nice." She scanned the parking lot. "Where's your car?"

"I walked," he said. "My house is less than five minutes from here."

"Well, then." She opened the driver door. "Get in. I'll give you a ride."

Even with the engine running the past few minutes,

the air conditioner had done little to cool off the car's interior. As she settled into the driver seat, she dropped the car's fob into a cup holder. While fastening her seat belt, she tried not to look at Brett. She tried not to think about what was going to happen next. Because, honestly, she wanted more from him than just a cup of coffee.

After a six-month-long romantic drought, it was no wonder that she was going home with the handsome pilot. But it was more than that. It seemed like her world had actually spun off its axis.

Her grandmother was her emotional support. After her mother left, it was Baba who put the little family back together. When her father remarried and moved to California while she was in college, she kept going back to Baba's house for holidays and breaks. The fact that her grandmother was now the one in need of care left her facing an uncomfortable truth. Nothing in life was certain beyond change.

Maybe that was why she wanted to go home with Brett. She was tired of playing by the rules and ready to really live—even if it was just for the night.

With an exhale, she put the gearshift into Drive and eased forward out of the space. "Which way?" she asked.

He pointed to a stop sign. "Go out of the parking lot over there."

Within minutes, she was parking her car next to the curb in front of a small house with a manicured lawn.

"Welcome to Casa de Brett," he said.

Pushing a button on her dashboard, she turned off the ignition. "You have a nice place," she said. "I've been in an apartment since moving to San Antonio—and that was almost eight years ago now. I'm never sure how I feel about home ownership."

"I bought this place three years ago, and I'll be honest, you're right to feel both." He paused. "Do you still want to come in?"

Without the engine running, the air-conditioning had turned off. The car's interior started to get warm. Sweat dampened her skin until her dress clung to her back. If she wanted to leave, now was the time. Lifting the fob from the cup holder, she slipped it inside the crossbody bag draped across her chest. "I don't work until noon, so I don't have to get up early."

After all, she could leave anytime she wanted. She'd agreed to a cup of coffee and nothing more. Yet, the kiss had awakened something deep inside of Eva— something that had been asleep for far too long—and reminded her that she was a woman with needs.

He slipped from the passenger seat and closed the door. Waiting at the curb, he lingered as she came to stand next to him. Reaching for her hand, he led her up the sidewalk.

Somehow, a swarm of butterflies had been let loose inside her, their wings beating against her belly. She hadn't felt this much nervous excitement in years, and the sensation left her giddy.

At the door, he entered a code into an electronic keypad. The latch unlocked with a click. He pushed the door open, and several interior lights began to glow.

Brett kicked off his shoes next to a mat. Eva did the same. The tile floor was cool under the soles of her feet. The air-conditioning had been set to polar, and the sweat dried, leaving gooseflesh on her arms. The front door opened to a living room, and a coffee table sat in the middle of the wooden floor. It was surrounded on three sides by a tan sofa and two matching chairs. A large TV hung on the wall.

"How do you take your coffee?" Brett turned left, passing through a dining room and into the kitchen.

Following behind him, she said, "Cream and sugar," before remembering her manners and adding, "please."

In the kitchen, he pulled a phone from his back pocket and set it on the counter. The device was inside a clear plastic case.

"I know this isn't any of my business," she said, picking up the cell, "but what gives?"

"Oh, that." He laughed. "A year or two ago, Wade had everyone over to his apartment complex for a cookout. There's a real nice pool, and we were all sort of goofing around. I ended up in the water and never thought to get rid of my phone before jumping in. Anyway, it ruined my phone and took forever to get all my information back." He picked up the phone and shook it. "Hence, the dry bag."

Wade was their mutual friend—the one who'd set them on the blind date. He was a new addition to San Antonio Medical Center's trivia team. After the first night joining the team at a local bar, she'd gotten to like Wade's sense of humor and eagerness for fun. She could well imagine a pool party gone awry. She also trusted him enough that when he told her that he knew the perfect guy, she let herself get fixed up with the pilot on his flight crew. Turns out, Wade had been right about Brett.

He was perfect for Eva.

She'd been quiet for a beat too long. Smiling up at him, she touched the waterproof pouch. "So, you have this just in case a crazy pool party breaks out."

"Yeah," he said. "Something like that."

A coffeepot sat on the counter next to the sink. A window looked out over the front yard, the sidewalk, the road and her car. He removed a container of decaf coffee from the fridge and scooped the grounds into a paper filter. "I don't have cream," he said, turning the maker on to brew. "I have skim milk or some kind of flavored creamer my sister left when she visited last month."

For Eva, flavored creamer was better. "That'll work."

As the earthy scent of fresh coffee filled the kitchen, Brett opened the refrigerator door. He stared at the shelves for a moment before reaching inside. "There it is." He held up a plastic container, handing it to her. "I think it's still good."

"This stuff keeps forever," she said, before reading the label. Yep, it'd be good for another three months. "Hazelnut. My favorite."

The simple domesticity of the situation hit her in the chest. She couldn't get wrapped up in thoughts of forever—or even tomorrow. There was only tonight. In the morning, well, a different set of problems already waited for her. But she'd worry about those then.

She moved closer to Brett, resting her hand next to his on the counter.

Stroking her pinky with his own, he said, "Seems like you're meant to be here."

"Seems like." A shiver of anticipation traveled up her arm.

He removed two mugs from the cabinet, setting them on the counter. The coffee maker hissed, spitting out the last drops. After picking up the full pot, he began to pour. "Tell me when."

"That's good," she said when the mug was nearly full. Flipping the lid, she opened the creamer and poured. Like liquid silk, cream swirled through the coffee, creating moving art. "Where do you keep your spoons?"

Brett opened a drawer and pulled out a spoon. He held it up. "Do you want anything else?"

Was there a bit of an invitation in his question, or was Brett just being a polite host? She took the spoon, letting her fingertips graze his palm. "Do you have sugar?"

From the same cabinet where he'd found the mugs, he pulled out a ceramic dish with a lid. He set it on the counter next to her. "I'm not judging," he said. "But even with decaf coffee, the sugar's going to keep you from getting any rest."

She stirred in a teaspoon of sugar and took a sip of coffee. Looking at him over the rim of her cup, she said, "Maybe I don't want to sleep."

"The night's long," he said, his voice smoky and filled with desire. "What do you plan to do with your time?"

She licked the spoon clean and set it on the counter, along with mug. "I was hoping that you had some ideas."

"I might be able to come up with something we can do."

"Oh yeah?" she asked, feeling flirty and powerful. "Like what? Maybe, this?"

She wrapped her arms around his waist and pulled him to her.

She claimed him with a hard kiss, which quickly turned more passionate than their first in the parking lot earlier. Eva opened her mouth, and Brett slipped his tongue between her lips. Like a storm cloud rolling across the plains, her thoughts darkened with worries. She shouldn't be here, not when her grandmother was in the hospital. No matter how much she wanted Brett— and she did want him—taking him as a lover was selfish.

Without any more thoughts, she stroked the front of his jeans. He was hard under her touch. She rubbed him through the fabric.

Kissing her deeper, he growled, "Damn it, Eva."

His words danced along her skin. She was going to do this and regret nothing. Shoving away the last of her worries, she unfastened the top button and pulled down on the zipper. She reached into his underwear and touched him, skin to skin.

Brett edged her back until her butt hit the kitchen counter. The scent of coffee hung in the air, mingling with the muskiness of their shared desire. He used a cord to lower the blinds over the front window. Then he stroked her breast, running his thumb over her nipple.

But she wanted to feel his touch on her flesh. She lowered a strap on her dress, along with the band of her bra, exposing herself to him. He traced her nipple with his thumb. Arching her back, she pressed herself into his hand. Lowering his head, he took her into his mouth. He sucked hard, before scraping his teeth over her breast.

Eva shuddered. Her skin was too tight, and she ached

with the need to have him inside of her. "Do you have protection?" she asked.

He removed his wallet from the back pocket of his jeans, then took out a foil packet. "Right here," he said, holding up the condom.

Reaching under her dress, Eva pulled down her panties, shimmying them to the floor. She kicked her underwear away as Brett tore the packet open and rolled the condom over his length. He lifted her up, resting her on the kitchen counter. Eva wrapped her legs around his middle, pulling him closer, and he entered her in one stroke.

Holding on to the counter's edge, she moved with Brett. The friction between them built. With one hand behind her back, he pulled her closer. As he claimed her mouth with his own, she knew what it meant to be alive and not simply exist. It didn't matter that she never slept with a guy this quickly—this moment would stay with her for a long time to come.

She felt an orgasm building, a tightening of her muscles. She was so close to her release. Reaching between their bodies, she found the top of her sex. She rubbed, and a shockwave curled her toes. She cried out as she came.

Brett kissed her again, driving into her hard and fast. She gripped his shoulders as he pumped his hips. Finally, he threw his head back and came as well. For a moment, they held each other. Her heart raced, and her breath was ragged.

He kissed her gently. "I'll be right back," he said.

Eva dropped to the ground. Her legs were wobbly. She held on to the counter to stay upright. "Of course."

"Give me a second." He held the front of his jeans together and hustled out of the kitchen.

She slipped into her panties. As she was straightening her dress, Brett returned. He reached for her hand. Pulling her to him, he wrapped his arms around her waist before touching his lips onto her own. "I won't be able to look at a cup of coffee for the rest of my life without thinking of you."

"Well, aren't you a charmer?" she teased.

In truth, he really was. He was smart, funny, and they shared an undeniable sexual chemistry. But what was she supposed to do next? Honestly, she didn't know if she should stay or go home.

Her mug sat on the counter. She dumped the coffee down the drain and set her spoon inside the cup, leaving both in the sink. "Well, I better..."

"You don't have to leave," he said, interrupting. "I mean, I'd like you to stay. But I understand if you... can't."

That old saying came to mind. *Wham! Bam! Thank you, ma'am!*

Okay, she didn't want to be one of those people.

Before she could say anything else, Brett added, "I make the best pancakes in the world. I can make you breakfast in the morning."

She chuckled. "First, you know of a restaurant with the best burritos in San Antonio. Now, you personally make the best pancakes in the whole world?"

"It's a hidden talent," he said before giving his wide smile.

Honestly, she didn't want to go anywhere, not now, at least. After all, she'd given herself permission to enjoy Brett for the night. And for her, the night was far from over.

Chapter 2

Hovering in the space between sleep and awakening, Eva knew that she was neither in her own apartment or even her own bed. The scent of pine, a male and the muskiness from sex hung in the air. The sheets were softer than the ones she used, and the room was cooler than she kept her bedroom.

Opening her eyes, she gazed at the man whose head lay on the pillow next to her. Brett's mouth was open slightly. He snored softly. His blond hair was tousled from sleep and last night's lovemaking.

Propping her head on her arm, she studied him as he slept. His cheeks were covered with a sprinkling of golden hair. Brushing her fingertips on his stubble, she recalled his breath on her shoulder. His lips were the color of a rich, red wine. Then came another memory, of his mouth on her thigh. Heat surged through her veins.

And now what? She wasn't sure what to do.

Roll over and go back to sleep?

Wake him and ask for the promised breakfast?

Leave without saying a word?

Sure, the last option wasn't classy. But it seemed to be the easiest.

At least she'd put her panties back on after their last round of lovemaking. She was also wearing Brett's undershirt. Sitting up, she scanned the room. Clothes—his and hers—littered the floor. Slipping from beneath the blankets, she padded quietly across the carpeting. Scooping up the entire pile—she could figure out what was hers later—she entered the adjacent bathroom.

After closing the door, she dropped all the clothes to the floor. It took her only seconds to find last night's outfit and get dressed. To be nice, she refolded all of Brett's belongings and set them next to the sink.

Looking up, she caught her reflection in a mirror that hung on the wall. The signs were unmistakable. Her dark hair fell in a tangled mess over her shoulders. Her brown eyes were bright. Her lips were swollen from being kissed. Her cheeks were red from where stubble had rubbed against her skin. She also had a stupid smile on her face—the kind that only came after—well, she came.

After winding her hair into a knot at the back of her neck, she used an elastic band from her pocket to secure a messy bun. She looked presentable enough to drive home. Now, there really was nothing more for her to do—other than leave.

Opening the door slowly, she stepped into Brett's room and grabbed her purse. She found her phone and glanced at the screen.

It was 5:37 a.m.

She'd missed fifteen calls.

Fifteen calls?

Her stomach dropped, and immediately she thought of her grandmother.

Scrolling through the log, she saw that the first call had come in at 3:45 a.m. The last, only moments ago. They were all from Katya. As children, the sisters had been best friends. In fact, they were still close, texting each other while simultaneously streaming true-crime documentaries. It didn't matter that their lives were different. Katya was married with kids and lived in the same community where the sisters had grown up. Eva had moved to San Antonio for work. She'd never married, and she didn't have kids. Hell, she didn't even have a goldfish.

She glanced back at her phone, and a single tear leaked down her cheek. Katya wouldn't have called so many times unless it was with bad news. Eva's eyes burned with tears she wanted to cry.

But she refused to get emotional in Brett's bedroom and while he was asleep, no less.

Anything her sister had to say could wait another few minutes. She'd call Katya back as soon as she got into her car. Before she could leave, she first had to find her shoes. Carefully lifting the corner of the bedspread, she peered under the bed frame.

No shoes.

The phone in her hand began to vibrate with an incoming call from Katya. After sending it to voicemail, she sent a text. I'll call you in two minutes. Sorry.

Then, she typed out another message:

What's going on with Baba?

Katya immediately replied.

You can't talk now? At least you're alive.

Her shoulders sagged. Of course, Katya would be concerned when she hadn't heard from Eva last night. That was what happened when you watched too many murder shows. What made matters worse, everyone in Encantador had been upset by the serial killer Decker Newcombe, who'd terrorized the community. Twice, the murderer had brought carnage to the small town.

She tapped out a message.

I'll call you in a minute.

She hit Send.

"Morning." Brett's voice was deep and husky.

The word landed in her middle.

Rubbing his eyes, he sat up. The blanket pooled across his lap, exposing his broad shoulders and well-defined pecs. A love bite that she'd given him had turned into a bruise.

Her face flamed with the memory. She hitched her purse onto her shoulder. "I didn't mean to wake you."

"Looks like you're heading out. I guess you decided to take a rain check on those pancakes."

The thing was, their date had turned into a good night—no, make that an excellent night. But she didn't know him, not really. Everything was flipped upside down. She'd always been told that after she met someone, a friendship should develop. Once she felt secure with that relationship, and then, only if the chemistry was unmistakable, should she have sex. At least, that was how it always had worked for her in the past.

With Brett, though, it had begun the other way around, and that just felt wrong.

Holding up her phone, she said, "I've missed a bunch of calls. I need to find out what's going on." She looked around the room. Bed. Dresser. TV on a stand. Bookcase. "I just can't find my damned shoes."

He scooted across the mattress and stood. Brett wore only his boxers, and she drank in the sight of him. Those broad shoulders. That muscular chest with chiseled abs. The line of hair that led straight down the front of his shorts. They were all too tempting for her own good. She was vaguely aware that once again this man was able to distract her from her troubles.

"You took them off by the front door," he said.

His words snapped her out of her fantasy. "I what?"

"Your shoes. You left them by the door."

He was right. She had. "Thanks. Well, I better..."

"I can still make you some pancakes," he offered, walking toward her. He was so close that she could reach out and touch him.

She wrapped both hands around her phone, squeezing tight.

He continued, "I like to think of myself as a man who keeps his promises."

Her phone vibrated with another text.

Are you okay?

What's the name of your first pet?

Her heart thudded. That question was their go-to incase either one was ever in trouble. It didn't necessarily mean something bad had happened, just that Katya wasn't about to give up until they spoke. "I really have to see what's going on with all these calls."

He smiled. "All right, then," he said, then paused. "At least let me walk you to the door." He looked down at the floor. "Any idea where my T-shirt went?"

"Uh, yeah. I slept in it. I changed in the bathroom. It's on the counter with all your other clothes."

"All my other clothes?" he echoed.

How was she supposed to explain that one? "Umm…"

"You know what, never mind." After walking to his dresser, Brett opened a drawer. He took out a pair of sweatpants and pulled them on. Then, he slipped a fresh T-shirt over his head. She had to admit, he looked almost as good dressed as he did in his underwear. He gave her a tight-lipped smile. "C'mon. I'll see you out."

They walked from the bedroom, along the hallway, down a set of stairs and through the living room. She wasn't sure what to say but was equally unhappy with the silence. In the tiled foyer by the front door, her sandals sat near the wall. She slipped them onto her feet.

Brett rested his hand on the door handle. "I'm not sure what happens next. Do I kiss you goodbye? Should I shake your hand?"

She gave a quick laugh and closed the distance between them. "How about a hug?"

"Deal." He opened his arms and she stepped into his embrace. God, it felt good to have him hold her. "Are you sure you don't want to stay for breakfast? After everything, well, it seems like I should do more than just give you a hug and say goodbye."

She inhaled his scent. He smelled like pine and mountain air. The thing was, she really was tempted to stay a little longer. But would they be able to navigate a new relationship after having had sex? "Maybe I can…"

The phone in her hand vibrated with an incoming call. She glanced at the screen. It was Katya. She sent it to voicemail. The phone began to ring again a moment later. Now Eva was getting a little nervous. Katya was a worrier, but something bad *might* have happened.

Exhaling, she slipped out of the embrace. "I really do need to see what's up."

"I get it." This time, when he reached for the handle, he opened the door.

She stepped outside. The sun had yet to rise over the horizon, and the street was quiet.

"Well…" She was struck with the urge to pull him to her and place her lips on his. Maybe he'd give her some privacy to call her sister back. Then she could stay for those pancakes he kept talking about. The phone in her hand began to shimmy.

"Looks like you really do have to take that," Brett said.

She stepped off the stoop. "Thanks again for everything."

"I hope it all works out for you." He lifted his hand in a small wave.

Phone still vibrating, she hustled to her car, where she took the call on her in-car audio. "What has gotten you so worked up? You knew I was going to call you back."

"You said you'd call me back in a minute," Katya snapped. "I was worried."

According to her phone, it had been eight minutes since first texting her sister. "I was going to call you as soon as I could."

She glanced at Brett's house. The front door was closed. She pulled away from the curb, taking the same route she had the night before, only in reverse.

"Are you in the car?" Katya asked. Did her sister's voice hold an accusatory tone? "Why are you out so early in the morning?"

"I *am* a nurse," she said, not wanting to tell her sister about the tryst. "We do work overnight shifts sometimes…"

"Last thing you told me, you had a date. You never called me when you got home. I was thinking that maybe the guy was a serial killer or something." Katya paused a beat. "Sorry you had to work and didn't get to go out. With everything going on, I just got worried that something happened to you, too."

Eva rubbed her forehead as she drove. Katya was taking care of a lot. The least she could do was acknowledge that her sister cared. "Thanks for looking out for me. How's Baba?"

"We had a rough night."

Approaching a stop sign, Eva let her foot off the gas and dropped it to the brake. Her heartbeat thrummed, echoing in her ears. "What happened?"

"I got a call from the hospital. She tried to get out of bed by herself and fell again." Katya exhaled a sob. "She's refusing to stay in the hospital, and honestly, I don't know what to do."

A wave of shock rolled through Eva. She needed to

say something, but her lips had gone numb. She still remembered her grandmother saying, *Home isn't a place, it's the people who love you most.*

Rolling through the intersection, Eva cleared her throat. "Is she okay now? Did she break any bones?"

"This time she's fine. But who knows what will happen when she tries to get out of bed again? And I know she'll keep trying."

They really were lucky that their grandmother wasn't seriously injured.

"How is she?"

Katya said, "Right now, she's sleeping. I've been here all night. When I realized that you hadn't checked in after your date, I got worried. I guess I should've known that you were working."

Eva's omission of the truth sat heavy in her gut. "You're a good sister. A great granddaughter and a fabulous mother," she said, "Go home. Get some rest. We can talk later."

"Before you hang up, the doctor wants to have a meeting with us. He scheduled it for this afternoon at two. You should be able to get down here in plenty of time…"

"My shift starts at noon."

"And you're just leaving the hospital now?"

"What? No…"

"You said that you were leaving work."

Damn. She hadn't exactly lied to her sister. But she had let her believe something that wasn't true. "Listen, I'm on the schedule for the next few days."

"Aren't there other nurses who can cover your shift?" Katya protested.

She didn't have any extra leave to use after taking time off a few weeks back. Her head started to ache. "The hospital's short-staffed at the moment."

Katya huffed. "I was really hoping for more support from you."

"What's that supposed to mean?"

"Well, like you said, you *are* a nurse. You'd understand everything the doctor will tell us."

Her sister had a point. Eva braked at a red traffic signal.

"I'll see about taking my break during the meeting," said Eva. "Then, I can call in to the meeting."

"That'd help a ton, thanks." She could hear the relief in Katya's voice.

Honestly, Eva was happy to be helpful. "Anything else?"

"Right now, Baba's in the hospital for observation. After a few days, she'll have to go somewhere. The doctor's hinting that the 'somewhere' is an elder care facility."

"I can't imagine she likes that idea at all," Eva said before asking, "What does she want to do?"

Katya gave a mirthless laugh. "She refuses to live anywhere but her own home. Jorje said she could live with us—even though it'd be tight. I mean, five of us already live in a three-bedroom house. But Baba doesn't want to live with me. And she doesn't want to go to the senior care facility, either."

"Sounds like our grandmother—stubborn and single-minded."

"Yes, it does," said Katya. "I'll talk to you at two." And then, she ended the call.

Still waiting for the traffic light to change, Eva glanced at the clock on her dashboard. It read 5:58 a.m. Not even 6:00 a.m., and already her day had been more eventful than the entire last week.

Her phone pinged with an incoming text. Would Katya just let up? Eva pulled over to the side of the road and glanced at the screen.

The message was from Brett. Her pulse raced.

Did you take care of your call?

She smiled. He really was a great guy. She typed out a reply.

Looks like it might be complicated.

He sent another text right away.

I'm good at complicated. Want to meet for lunch before you go to work? We can talk about it. I know a place that has excellent burgers.

He was charming and persistent. She started to reply:

What time?

Her thumb hovered above the Send icon. She liked Brett, truly. They were certainly compatible—both in bed and out. She could still feel his kisses on her lips. Her cheeks were rubbed raw by the stubble on his chin.

But her life might be *too* complicated, even for a second date. There was her grandmother to think about.

A solution as to where the older woman could live had taken root in Eva's mind. It would be a big commitment on her part, so until she was ready, she wouldn't broach the idea to anyone—not even Katya.

If everything in her life was about to change, then she really couldn't start a new relationship.

She deleted her unsent message, typed out a new one and hit Send. Before she pulled away from the curb, she glanced at her reply still visible on her phone screen... and felt how final it was.

I had a great time last night, but I can't see you again. Sorry.

Chapter 3

Golden light streamed through a set of French doors that led to a backyard patio. A TV hung on the wall. Images flickered across the screen, though the sound was muted. In the kitchen, the coffee maker gurgled as it brewed. Sitting on the sofa in his living room, Brett read the text from Eva. His gut clenched with disappointment. How had he gotten her signals so wrong?

At least she was being honest at the outset. No need to waste time wondering if their first date would lead to a second one—or even a relationship.

Eva was a sexy woman who also happened to be a generous and passionate lover. But there was more to like about her than just the physical. She was smart, funny and interesting. In short, she was a rare combination of everything he wanted in a partner.

So yeah, it sucked that she didn't even want to give it a try.

Picking up the phone, he looked at the screen. The message was still there, mocking him.

I had a great time last night, but I can't see you again. Sorry.

There was nothing else for him to do besides forget that he'd ever met Eva Tamke.

The thing was, he didn't want to forget.

He checked the time. It was 6:14 a.m.

Damn. He hadn't been up this early since his days as a warrant officer in the army.

Rubbing his eyes, he wondered what he was supposed to do next. Sure, he could go back to bed for a few more hours of shut-eye. But after what happened, he doubted that he'd get much rest. Since he didn't have to be at work until 2:00 p.m., he had an entire day to fill.

Rising from the sofa, he padded into the kitchen. He filled a cup to the rim with coffee from the pot. He took a sip and let the caffeine buzz through his system.

Last night, he'd made a pot of decaf coffee that he and Eva had barely touched. She took her coffee with flavored creamer and sugar—more of a dessert than a drink. The sugar dish still sat on the counter. Her mug was in the sink. Lipstick ringed the spoon's neck where she'd licked it clean. Funny, she'd only been in his house a few hours. Now, it seemed like everything reminded him of her.

Coffee cup in hand, he returned to the sofa. Leaning back into the cushions, he looked at his phone. He'd missed a call from Gus, the newly hired flight nurse on the air ambulance's crew. Gus had left a message in the middle of the night. "Hate to bother you. But I have a work question. It's important. Call me back."

Brett didn't typically call people so early in the morning. But Gus had said it was important. Using the number from the message, he placed a call.

Gus answered after the second ring. "Hey, Brett." The dude's voice was raspy and weak. "Thanks for calling me back."

"No offense, my man. But you don't sound too good."

"No offense taken. My kid came home from school with the stomach bug. Everyone at home caught it. This is my first time taking a personal day. I'm not sure of the protocol."

"Usually, you call Darla at human resources. She's in charge of finding replacements for the flight crew." There was no need to make a sick man deal with requesting leave time. He continued, "I'll reach out and let her know. I hope everyone is healthy soon."

"You and me both," said Gus.

After hanging up, he placed another call.

It was answered after the second ring. "This is Darla."

"To be honest," said Brett, by way of greeting, "I'm impressed that you're at work already."

"Make that still," said Darla with a wry laugh. "And I'm impressed that you're awake at all."

"Well, I got an email. Gus is out with a stomach bug, and that means…"

Darla finished his thought. "You need someone to fill in until he comes back." She tapped on a keyboard. "A nurse with experience working on a medevac helicopter will be difficult to find on such short notice. But I'm on it," she added, ending the call.

Before he had the chance to set down his phone, it pinged with an incoming text. His pulse spiked. Was it Eva? He hoped like hell that she'd reconsidered his offer for a lunch date. Or any date, really. He glanced at the screen.

The message was from his sister, Shannon.

Text me when you get up. I need help brainstorming...

Brett groaned. He loved his sister, but he knew that an early-morning text was probably bad news. Right now, her life was difficult. She was in the middle of a messy divorce. Her soon-to-be-ex, Lucian, owned several car dealerships in the Dallas/Ft. Worth area. As it turned out, not all of his deals were legit. What was worse, his shady activities spilled into his personal life. Shannon had given Lucian more chances than Brett could count because she always wanted to work things out for their kids—four-year-old twins, Paige and Palmer.

Instead of texting his sister, he placed a call. She answered after the first ring.

"Wow. It's not like you to be up this early."

"So I've heard." He wasn't going to tell his sister about Eva, especially since the relationship had crashed during takeoff. He paused before asking, "What's up?"

Shannon drew in a shaking breath. "It's Lucian. He hasn't paid for the preschool program. And if he doesn't pay..."

Her words unwound, like a spool of thread rolling across the floor. He knew his sister couldn't afford it on her own. If the kids weren't in preschool, they'd need childcare, which also cost money. She'd end up relying on Lucian, which was what the jerk wanted. To control the situation. Honestly, Brett wasn't surprised. Mad, yes. Shocked, no.

"Bad day for me not to have childcare," Shannon said. "I have an interview this morning for a bank job with more room for professional growth."

He knew his sister had had to ask their parents for financial help, and sitters were hard to come by at a moment's notice. If Dallas wasn't a full five hours from San Antonio, he'd offer to watch the kids.

"I'll pay the tuition," he said without hesitation. True, he'd paid the retainer for her divorce attorney. That check had wiped out his rainy-day fund. But he had cash enough to help his sister. After turning on the phone's speaker function, he opened a payment app. "If I can transfer the money directly to the school, I'll pay now. How much do you need?"

Shannon gave him the school's pay-share address, along with the amount.

He sucked in a breath. "That's more than my whole mortgage payment."

"I know. I know," said Shannon. "I'm going to have to switch them to something more affordable—unless Lucian starts to pay. But there's so much chaos right now. I just want their lives to be close to normal."

"I get it," he said. "I want what's best for my nieces, too." He typed the amount into the app, along with a note that it was for Paige and Palmer's account. Then, he transferred the money. "Done. And don't worry about paying me back."

"Thank you, Brett. You're really the best. Whoever ends up with you will be the luckiest lady alive."

Eva's face flashed through his mind. Rubbing the back of his neck, he tried to laugh. Even he could hear the tension in his voice. "Well, I probably won't meet her today."

"I better get going," said his sister.

"Good luck with everything. Let me know how it goes."

"Will do," she said. Then she ended the call.

Setting the phone down, he leaned back into the sofa. It wasn't even 6:30 a.m. Already, he'd had quite a day.

His phone pinged again with a new message.

He knew it wouldn't be Eva. Still, hope like an electric current ran through him.

It was a notification from the bank informing him of his new balance. Brett cursed. In helping his sister, he'd almost wiped out his account. True, being flat-ass broke was only temporary. Next week, he'd get a paycheck. But he hadn't meant to give away all his money.

Holding his thumb on the power button, he turned off his phone. The last thing he wanted was another early-morning text. Especially, since the universe seemed to be conspiring against him.

It wasn't like him to be pessimistic. But he knew why he was so sullen.

He hated to admit it, but Eva's rejection still stung. Her scent filled his home. The taste of her lingered on his lips. Yet, the relationship was over before it had begun. The real kicker was, he didn't know why.

Well, he wasn't going to sit here and think about it anymore. They'd had one hell of the night, and for whatever reason, she was done.

So he was he.

* * *

Decker Newcombe lay in a hospital bed and tried to focus. It was hard to think around the constant beeping of the machines and the dullness caused by the pain meds. The bed, which he rarely left, shifted every few hours to prevent bedsores. The disinfectant scent of manufactured pine, stale coffee and his own body odor surrounded him like a fog.

The last things he remembered clearly were smoke and fire. He'd been trapped in an inferno. The pain had been unrelenting and unbearable. In the moment, he was certain that his sins had finally caught up with him and he'd been dragged to hell.

As it turned out, he hadn't been that lucky.

He'd been brought to a hospital in San Antonio, which he figured was its own kind of hell. Hours, days and weeks melted together until he couldn't tell how long he'd been handcuffed to the bed. Time didn't flow like a river but rather rushed in and receded like an ocean's tide.

Still, he knew a bit about what was happening to him and why. The information came through snatches of conversation he overheard while nurses and doctors talked with the police officer posted outside his door.

As much as he hated to have a cop sitting outside his hospital room, in a way, he was flattered. It meant the police still viewed him as a threat—and he most certainly was. Even before Decker knew that he was a direct descendant of Jack the Ripper, a Victorian-era serial killer, he was a dangerous man.

Decker had plotted the ultimate murder, a crime that

he was to commit live on the internet. It would make him the most famous killer of all time.

Things hadn't gone according to plan.

There'd been a fire in the warehouse where he was set up to stream the killing. A fight with his former friend and now ultimate enemy, Ryan Steele, left them both bloodied and bruised. In the end, he'd been shot by the undersheriff from Encantador, Kathryn Glass.

Certainly, they could've left him for dead, but the undersheriff and Ryan had pulled him out of the blaze. Then they'd called paramedics, who gave him medical care and transported him to a hospital. As a man comfortable with vengeance, he couldn't fathom their thinking when they decided to save his life.

A normal man would feel gratitude.

Decker felt nothing.

No, that wasn't true. In those first days after the fire, he felt gut-wrenching agony. Whenever the meds wore off, there was a pounding in his left side with every beat of his heart. His lungs had burned with each breath. His right hand and arm had felt as if they were still on fire.

But since he had nothing to do but lie in bed and think, more memories returned.

The hacker who'd helped him—a person he knew only as Seraphim—had sent him a message.

You have a son with Anastasia Pierce.

Along with the message was a picture of the birth certificate. On it, Decker was listed as the father.

Memories of Ana haunted him like a ghost. A dozen

years ago, they had lived together for ten months. True, he'd been working as muscle for hire the whole time— strong-arming people who owed money to a loan shark. But with her, he'd almost felt normal. It was the one time in his life that he dared to have hope for some kind of future. For him, Ana was a single ray of sunshine breaking through the clouds of a raging storm that was his soul.

Then, one day, he came home, and she was gone. She'd taken all her things, even the kitten he'd given her. She'd left him with the furniture, the dishes.

He still remembered the date it happened. Seven months before the birth certificate had been issued.

It didn't take a genius to figure out what had happened. Ana discovered she was pregnant and split. But the fact that she didn't want him involved with the kid hurt worse than all his other injuries combined.

Yet, she'd listed him as the father.

There'd always been an underlying goodness to Ana. She might have been finished with Decker, but she wouldn't lie about her child's paternity.

Since he had nothing to do with his time but think, he realized that the hacker might've been lying to him from the beginning. But what would Seraphim gain by lying? They wanted to spread chaos and had chosen Decker to help them. After finding Decker through an internet café, they offered to fund his next killing—so long as Decker was willing to murder his victim live and on the internet.

Since Decker was determined to be the most famous serial killer of all time, he was in on the plan.

Which brought him back to the original question.

Why would Seraphim lie to Decker about something like a child?

Then again, Seraphim was a weird person. They hid their identity behind a long-beaked plague doctor mask. Their voice was always distorted by electronics.

Decker's computer had surely burned up in the warehouse fire. But he'd stashed a cell phone in Mexico with Seraphim's number. If he could get the phone, then he could ask the hacker to find out if the kid was really his.

How was he supposed to get out of the hospital and back to Mexico? He needed an escape plan. But his whole body throbbed like a bass drum. It must be time for more meds.

"You going in there?" a male voice came from the hallway. It was the cop who guarded his door, Officer Kwan. Over time, Decker had come to recognize the different voices.

"It's happy hour," a female said. Nancy, the afternoon nurse, was always glib. The happy hour she referred to was Decker's cocktail of medications.

"I guess you heard the news?" asked Kwan.

"No, what news?"

"The doc says he's healthy enough to leave San Antonio Medical Center. He's getting transferred to a jail hospital."

Nancy said, "Honestly, I'm not surprised. His vitals are looking good. Do you know when he's leaving?"

"Soon," said Kwan. "This morning I was told that I don't have to come back tomorrow. But before they're sending him to jail, he's headed to Encantador for a hearing."

Decker heard the door open, and he looked over. Nancy was holding the door with her back, now saying something to the cop about the weather. He could see the toe of Officer Kwan's shoe. It was shiny, black and reflected the overhead lights.

So, he was going back to Encantador. That was an interesting twist. But how could he use it to his advantage?

With the soles of her sneakers squeaking on the tile floor, Nancy pivoted. Before she entered the room, Decker let his eyes drift closed.

"It's time for the fun meds," she said.

He didn't reply. He never did.

The smell of rubbing alcohol filled the room. "This might feel cold," she said, wiping his arm. "And here's a pinch."

He watched as she injected a solution into his IV tube. Cool liquid began to flow through his veins.

"I don't know why you talk to him," said Kwan. "He never replies."

"Well, I just want my patients to know that I'm here and I care." She patted the back of Decker's hand.

"Care?" the police officer snorted. "You know who this is, right? You've heard all about what he's done."

"It's not my job to pass judgment," she said. "Just to provide the treatment he needs." A moment passed, then she added, "There, all done." She left the room, the door closing behind her.

"Whatever," Decker heard Kwan say.

A phone pinged loudly with an incoming message. There was silence for a few seconds. "You won't have to worry about him too much longer," Kwan said at last.

"That text was from my boss. Looks like the feds are sending an agent to take custody of your patient."

"And then what?" Nancy asked. "They're going to drive him in a convoy?"

"Even better. Looks like he's getting taken by helicopter."

Good to know, you gabby idiots. The meds were trying to have their way with him, but Decker Newcombe was too mighty an opponent for anything coursing through his system. *Focus*, he ordered himself. *Remember what they said and make a plan.*

His mind started to fill with an image of a small boat floating atop the warm waters of the Gulf. Fluffy white clouds. A clear blue sky.

C'mon, you're Decker Newcombe. You've got things to do. Including finding out if you're a father.

He fought the fuzziness of the pain meds with everything he had.

And he had *a lot*. If he wanted to survive, he had to think. But how could he, when his head was filled with thick, white clouds and a soft blue sky? The sun was a bright, white ball. Then he was absorbed by the light and the pain was washed away by the tide.

Chapter 4

The sun hung in a cloudless sky over downtown San Antonio. Heat shimmered off the pavement in waves. Brett sat in the driver's seat of his pickup truck and glanced at the instrument panel. It was 1:50 p.m. Ten minutes early for his shift at the hospital.

The main campus for San Antonio Medical Center filled up several blocks to his left. As he stopped at an intersection, waiting for a break in traffic, his blinker gave off a hypnotic *tick-tick-tick*.

Usually, he was happy for his shift to begin. But today he wasn't.

Honestly, he'd tried to forget about Eva. It hadn't worked. There was something about her that had gotten to him. They'd made a connection, and while she clearly wasn't interested in pursuing it—and he respected her choice—he wished he could figure out what had gone wrong.

Pulling onto a road that ran adjacent to the hospital, he followed the blue sign to the medical flight facility. The road ended at a small parking lot. Beyond that was a domed metal hangar. It housed offices, held equip-

ment and, if necessary, because of severe weather, the
helicopter itself.

Brett pulled into a parking spot near the door. A metal
sign was affixed to a post: Reserved for Pilot in Command. He turned off the engine and stared out the windshield. The helicopter sat on the landing pad. It was
painted white, with SAMC's blue logo on the door.

As he did each time that he looked at his helicopter,
he knew he was a lucky guy.

He had a job he loved. His crew was more like family
than coworkers or even friends. But Eva's abrupt entry
and exit from his life stung. At least he'd get to fly today.
Maybe that was part of his problem. He was only truly
happy when he was in the air.

Without the truck's engine running, there was no air-
conditioning. The cab grew brutally hot. A bead of sweat
snaked down the side of his face, and he wiped it away
with his thumb. He opened the door, but it was no better.
An oven-like heat rolled over him in a wave.

As per regulations, he wore a flight suit. The fabric
was flame retardant, but the material didn't breathe.
Sweat ran down his back and pooled at the base of his
spine.

A yellow sports car entered the back of the lot. The
driver gave two quick blasts from the horn as it swerved
into a spot. Brett lifted his hand in greeting.

The door opened, and Wade Shaw, one of the two
EMTs on his crew, unfolded himself from the small car.
Before working as a flight EMT, Wade had played col-

lege basketball. The paramedic claimed to be six-eleven, and Brett believed him.

Wagging his finger, Wade approached. He also wore a flight suit. "You look like crap, no offense. It makes me think you had a very late night with my new friend, Eva Tamke."

Heading toward the hangar, Brett knew he had to be diplomatic. "She's a nice lady. We had a nice time."

"Nice lady?" Wade repeated. "Nice time? She's absolutely perfect for you. Did she tell you that she used to be in the air force? She even worked on a flight crew as a nurse."

"She was in the Air National Guard," Brett said, correcting his friend.

Wade shrugged his shoulders. "Same difference. When are you seeing her again?"

"We aren't going out on another date."

Wade stopped midstride, leaving Brett walking alone.

Brett glanced over his shoulder as he spoke. "She has some things going on in her life. I do, too."

"What's going on that's more important than finding your soulmate?"

"Soulmate?" Brett opened the door. Thankfully, the inside of the hangar was dark and cool. "That's assuming a lot." He paused a beat. "My bastard of a brother-in-law won't pay for his kids' tuition."

"I thought your nieces were little. Why do they need tuition?"

"Apparently, fancy preschool costs a lot—like more

than a house payment." Hopefully, it was enough information to move the subject away from last night's date.

"So, what does that have to do with Eva?"

He'd had lots of luck so far that day. Unfortunately, all of it had been bad.

He didn't want to get into what happened last night. Aside from the fact that the adage was true about discretion being the better part of valor and all. He didn't want to admit that the night had been great, but Eva didn't want anything more to do with him. He ignored Wade's question.

The rest of the crew was already at the flight facility. Stacy, the copilot, and Lin, the other EMT, sat on folding chairs at a table with thin metal legs. A line of cards ran down the middle of the table, a game of gin rummy already underway.

"It's too hot outside to do any preflight." Stacy said as Brett approached. "We got the game started."

The medevac crew worked nine-hour shifts, overlapping another two other crews to cover an entire day. On some shifts, the chopper was in the air more than it was on the ground. Those days were filled with flying some seriously injured or ill people to the hospital. But mostly, the worst part of the job was boredom. If there were no calls, the crew was left with little to do.

He said, "Gus is out sick. Darla's supposed to send his replacement. I've got some paperwork to fill out, then you can deal me into the game." Duffel bag in hand, he walked toward his small office at the rear of the hangar. "If the replacement nurse shows up, let me know."

His phone buzzed with an incoming text from Darla in HR. He read the message as he walked. Apparently, the crew was transporting a patient to a different facility. But first Brett had to talk to an FBI agent.

There were about a dozen things Brett had to worry about before getting his helicopter in the air. But only one thing mattered right now.

What in hell did the FBI want with him?

Eva stood next to a bed in the emergency department at San Antonio Medical Center. She read the LCD panel on the thermometer. The patient, a four-year-old girl, had a fever of one hundred and two. Lying on a bed, the child had a white blanket pulled up to her chin.

Eva picked up the tablet computer from the small workstation and entered the information into the intake form.

The girl's mother stood on the opposite side of the bed. "So?" she asked.

Smiling at the girl and her mom, she said, "Your daughter definitely has fever." Then, to the patient, she asked, "And your throat hurts, pumpkin?"

The girl nodded. "It hurts bad," she said, her voice raspy.

"A doctor is going to come in," she told the child. "He'll use a really big Q-tip to tickle the back of your throat." She suspected strep throat but wouldn't know until a test had been run. To the mom, she asked, "Has she been around anyone who's sick?"

"She just started preschool. It seems like everyone has a runny nose or a cough."

Eva gave the woman a sympathetic smile. "It's like that at the beginning of the school year."

"I tried to get her an appointment with her pediatrician, but they were booked for days. When, she stopped wanting to drink anything, I figured I couldn't wait."

"It's best to get checked out. We don't want a little something to become a big something," Eva said, assuring the mom that she'd made the right decision. "The doctor will be in shortly. If you need anything, let me know."

She left the exam room. A clock on the wall read 2:01 p.m. Her pulse jumped. How had the time gotten away from her? She was supposed to be on the call with Katya and Baba's doctor already. Each second slipped through her fingers.

The longer she thought about her plan, the more she liked it. She was going to move to Encantador and help take care of her grandmother.

True, there were things that she'd miss about living in San Antonio. She had a job and friends. But nothing tethered her to the community—not really. She wasn't like Brett; she hadn't bought a house. She didn't have kids in school or a partner who'd also have to relocate.

After talking to Katya and her grandmother, she would tell her coworkers. Then she'd put in her official notice.

The nurse's station was a long counter in the middle of a warren of beds and rooms. A lower counter served as a desk. It was always cluttered with papers, a desktop computer, tablets and several phones. The scent of disinfectant circulated on a constant stream of icy air.

Her coworker, Rex, stood behind the counter. He looked up as she approached. "What's the verdict?"

Setting the tablet on the counter, Eva said, "I'd bet it's strep, but the doc will have to give her a test."

Rex nodded. "I'll send him there next."

A Latino in his late fifties, Rex was like an uncle to many on the staff—Eva included. Earlier, she'd told him about her grandmother's fall and the call to discuss long-term care options. Rex understood that she wanted to be a part of the meeting, even if it was over the phone.

"Unless you need anything else, I'm going to step into the break room and call my sister," she said.

He gave her a warm smile. "I hope everything works out for your grandma."

"Me, too."

A phone on the desk began to ring. Rex sighed. "Hold up a minute, Eva. That's the internal hospital line. Let's see what's happening." Lifting the receiver to his ear, he said, "Emergency Department." He paused a beat and then said, "Yeah?" Brows drawn together, he cast a glance in her direction. "Sure, we can," he said before hanging up the phone. He turned to Eva. "That was Darla with HR. She called about you."

"Me?" Anxiety exploded in her middle, leaving her with too much energy. Was the call about Brett and their date? What if the hospital had a nonfraternization policy and someone had found out about their night together? "What did Darla want?"

"You're being reassigned for the rest of your shift."

"Reassigned?" She exhaled a long breath. So, the call had nothing to do with her one-night stand. "Sure, where do they need me?"

"At the heliport. Now."

"I'm not flight certified. Not anymore, at least."

Rex shook his head. "It doesn't matter. You worked on a helicopter when you were in the army."

"It was the Air National Guard," she corrected, "That was when I was in college, like, sixteen years ago."

"All's I know is that they're short-staffed and need a nurse. You got picked."

There were several medevac crews who worked for the hospital. What were the chances that Brett Wilson happened to be the pilot of this particular crew? "I'll head to the hangar after my call."

"No time for that," said Rex. "They need you now. They've been called out and can't take off without you."

She glanced at her phone. There were four messages, all from Katya. A sick feeling settled in her gut. Slipping the phone into her pocket, she said, "I'll go now."

"I knew we could count on you. They'll have a flight suit you can use." Rex gave her arm a squeeze. "I'll have Security give you a lift."

Hustling down a long hallway, Eva sent a text to her sister.

I've been reassigned for the day. I can't call in. I'm so sorry.

It didn't seem like she'd done enough. She sent another message.

I'll come down this weekend. See you Saturday.

Katya responded.

Baba has to stay at the hospital for a week, so we have some time. We'll talk when you get home.

A security guard, clad in a tan shirt and brown pants, waited next to the employee entrance. "You Eva?" she asked.

"I am."

"I'm Natalie and supposed to give you a lift. Follow me." The guard approached a set of glass doors that opened with a swish.

Eva stepped outside. The sun beat down onto the pavement. In seconds, sweat streamed down the back of her scrubs.

Since the hospital complex was larger than a professional sports stadium, security guards drove official golf carts and provided rides to patients and employees alike. One of those carts, painted white with the blue SAMC logo on the hood, waited at the curb.

Natalie got behind the steering wheel. Eva followed and slipped into the passenger seat. "Thanks for the ride."

"Hold on," the guard ordered. "I've been told to get you to the flight facility STAT."

As the cart lurched forward, Eva grabbed a metal bar that was attached to the dashboard. They jostled through the parking lot and down a side road. It took only minutes before the cart rolled to a stop near the door to the hangar.

A white helicopter was on the landing pad. A blond woman wearing a flight suit sat in the pilot's seat.

Honestly, Eva wasn't sure if she were relieved or disappointed that the pilot wasn't Brett. Nodding her thanks to the guard, she hopped down.

The woman in the helicopter looked up and smiled as Eva approached. "You must be our nurse."

Sun reflected off the white aircraft and the concrete tarmac. It made looking at the woman painful. Shading her eyes with her hand, she said, "Eva Tamke."

"My name's Stacy Janowitz. Nice to meet you. We got a call right after the shift change, so we're scrambling to get into the air. Go inside the hangar and ask one of the guys for a flight suit. You'll need to change quick so we can get off the ground."

Inside, a man with black hair stood next to a bank of metal lockers. Eva smiled and walked toward him. "I spoke to your pilot, Stacy. She said someone in here would have a flight suit for me." She paused. "Sorry, I should've introduced myself first. I'm Eva Tamke, the nurse."

The man said, "We really appreciate you filling in at the last minute. I'm Lin, one of the EMTs." He opened the door to a locker where a flight suit hung on a peg. He handed her the uniform and pointed to the rear of the hangar. "There's a bathroom back there. You can use it to change."

"Thanks. I'll be ready in a minute, then Stacy can take off."

She started across the long, cavernous room. Like she told Rex, it had been more than a decade since she'd been part of a helicopter crew. She didn't miss flying, per se. But she was excited to get back in the air, and adrenaline coursed through her veins.

As she headed for the bathroom, she could see someone sitting behind a desk in an office with a long narrow window in the door.

Someone very familiar.

And because she was staring at Brett Wilson, he happened to look up. Her eyes locked with his, and the breath caught in her chest.

He stood, and she pushed open the door and stepped inside. "Is it too cheesy to ask what a nice guy like you is doing in a place like this?"

"I work here and happen to like the flight facility." He cleared his throat. "So, I guess the real question is—why are *you* here?"

She refused to let him unsettle her. Standing taller, she said, "Darla said the medevac needed a nurse with flight experience."

Resting his elbows on the desk, he laced his fingers together. Despite his less than enthusiastic greeting, she still found him handsome. He gazed at her with his deep blue eyes, and her pulse raced.

He cleared his throat. "I'm glad to see that we've got a nurse. From what you said last night, it sounds like you still remember the job."

He was right. But there were other things she remembered, as well. Like the feeling of his lips on hers. Or how she fit perfectly next to him in the bed. If all she could think about was the feeling of his hands on her skin, then maybe it was best if she didn't work with the helicopter crew after all.

"I'm not sure that this is the best idea—me and you working together, I mean." She winced as soon as the last word left her mouth. She hadn't meant to be so candid. But working with Brett was the last thing she should do.

She was needed, though, and there was no going back now.

Brett worked his jaw back and forth. "I don't think we have the luxury of you accepting this assignment or not. We have to transport a patient. I'm not completely sure what's going on." Before he could say any more, the phone on his desk began to ring. "Stay there for a minute. Let me get this, then we can talk."

"I'll give you some privacy." She stepped into the hangar, just outside of the office door.

Brett picked up the call. "This is Brett Wilson."

A voice came across on the phone's speaker, loud enough that she could clearly hear. "This is Jason Jones. I'm a supervisory special agent with the FBI office here in San Antonio, calling regarding the patient you're about to transport."

Why was the FBI calling about this patient? Maybe the less she knew about the call, the better. She took a few steps back, creating more distance between herself and the phone.

The FBI agent spoke again, and she froze. "You're going to be taking a patient from SAMC. I've got to warn you, this person is particularly dangerous. Because of the risks, we've chosen to transport them via air ambulance to cut down on travel time."

"Okay." Brett's tone was wary. "What else can you tell me?"

Eva took a step back. She shouldn't be listening to a call between Brett and an FBI agent. But then the agent spoke, and she stopped her retreat.

"The hospital you'll be going to is in a small town south of you. It's called Encantador."

Her pulse started to race. The helicopter was headed to the hospital where her grandmother was also a patient. It didn't matter what else the agent had to say. It didn't matter that she was a fool for tempting herself by being around Brett, a man she wanted but would never get to have again.

Pressing the flight suit to her chest, she hustled toward the bathroom. After opening the door, she closed and locked it. Leaning against the wall, she drew in a single deep breath.

Being part of the crew would get her exactly what she needed—the ability to see her grandmother.

Yet, she needed to stay away from Brett. Even moreso, since her rejection of him this morning. She really couldn't develop feelings for anyone with so much going on in her life right now. Working with him was going to make it that much harder to keep her feelings neutral.

She drew in a single, deep breath.

She could still refuse to take the assignment.

No. She wouldn't let the hospital down by bringing

her personal life to work. Exhaling fully, she stripped out of her scrubs and worked her feet into the legs of the flight suit.

After all, she just had to work with Brett for a few hours. What could really happen in such a short time?

Chapter 5

Brett had just gotten off the call with the FBI agent, and he didn't like the situation one bit. Jones had explained who they were transporting. Brett always thought he'd seen and heard it all, that little could faze him.

He was wrong.

He knew that declining the assignment was an option. Not even the feds could force him to fly if he thought it was unsafe. But even though he was in charge of the aircraft, he liked his crew to be a democracy. Every person got a vote if the situation was difficult.

And damn, but this was one of the most difficult transports he'd ever make.

More than their notorious patient, it seemed that Eva had changed her mind about staying for the shift while he was on the call. Now, she was dressed in a flight suit. He couldn't help but wonder why she'd made a different decision, even though it shouldn't matter to him.

Still, he had a job to do. Up first was briefing his crew. They were all gathered near the folding table. He took a moment to look everyone in the eye. Wade. Stacy. Lin. He met Eva's gaze last. Despite it all, his gut tightened.

The baggy jumpsuits were made for function, not

fashion. But even the bland fabric seemed to give her skin a glow, even though it hid curves he knew lay beneath.

His fingers itched with the memory of tracing the outline of body after they'd had sex the second time. Or maybe it had been after their third round. How was he supposed to work with her and pretend like he didn't know her intimately? Hell, her scent still clung to his skin.

Then again, he knew what had to be done.

He couldn't look at her as a woman he desired. He had to see her as a colleague and a member of his crew. As hard as it was, he refocused his gaze.

She still had her hospital ID hanging around her neck. She'd have to remove it before they were airborne. But other than that, she looked ready to work. He wasn't sure why she'd changed her mind about staying on the crew for the shift, but he certainly wasn't going to question her now. After the phone call with Special Agent Jones, Brett needed to focus on the mission.

"We're about to take a patient from the hospital. I want you to know what you're getting into before you step onto the aircraft." He paused. "I assume you've all heard the name Decker Newcombe."

It was an easy assumption to make. The serial killer had been in the news for years. The media became fascinated with him when he assassinated a district attorney in Wyoming and then escaped arrest by living off the grid. He'd reemerged and killed four people in southern Texas around Christmas, then continued his killing spree throughout the region. A few weeks ago, he'd been taken into custody following a botched murder that he'd planned to stream live on the internet. The murderer was injured during the ensuing chaos and then taken into custody.

"Well, Mr. Newcombe has been recovering from his injuries at SAMC. He's due to be officially charged with all his crimes later today. Then, he'll be taken to jail, where he'll finish recovering at the hospital there. The feds want him transported via medevac, and that's where we come in." Tension pinched his shoulders together, and he rubbed the back of his neck. "I don't like this at all, although I've been assured that the patient will be restrained. Plus, he'll be guarded by a US marshal the whole time. Questions?"

Lin lifted a hand. "Can we refuse?"

"I suppose we can," he said.

Lin continued, "I mean, we aren't police officers. We've transported some rowdy patients, but this is different."

The safety and well-being of his crew—both physical and emotional—was his top priority. It meant making sure they were all willing to fly, regardless of the circumstances. "That's why I wanted to talk with you all before we take off."

"I don't know about any of you," said Lin, "but I don't want to fly a serial killer around."

Wade countered with, "We've had dangerous people in the chopper before."

"Dangerous, sure. But deranged?" Lin shrugged.

"I hate to tell the hospital no," said Stacy, "especially

since we're the only helicopter crew on right now. Can't the Texas Rangers take him?"

It was one of the things that Brett had brought up with SSA Jones. "They don't have anything with the medical equipment we have."

"We should vote," said Wade. "I'm a yes."

"No," said Lin.

"What about you, Stacy?" he asked.

She puffed out her cheeks before blowing out a long breath. "I'd like to have more time to think about this." She paused. "What would happen if we refused?"

"I guess transporting the prisoner becomes the feds' problem." He'd tried to keep from looking at Eva, if only because his pulse raced every time he saw her. But he turned to her now. "You've been quiet. What do you think?"

"I'm not really part of this crew," she said. "I'm just filling in for the day."

"But if we take off, you'll be on the helicopter. That means that you get a say-so."

She inhaled and exhaled. "You said that Decker Newcombe will be restrained. You said that a US marshal will be on board."

She hadn't really asked him any questions. Yet Brett said, "Correct to both."

"I'm still not sure if I should vote," she said. "But Decker Newcombe is one man who's going to be restrained. Plus, he's going to be guarded. I'm sure the marshal is trained to keep the situation under control."

"Handle him?" Lin echoed. "He's a killer."

"But he's also a patient," she said.

The list of things he liked about Eva was already long. Now, he had to add two more characteristics. She was brave and committed to her job.

"I guess I'm a yes, too," said Stacy.

"Majority rules," said Brett. "We need to be ready to take off in fifteen minutes. But, Lin, I won't make you go if you aren't comfortable."

Folding his arms across his chest, the EMT exhaled loudly. "I'm not happy, but I'm also not going to let y'all take off without me. I'm in."

"We need to be vigilant during this mission," Brett said. "But we always have to be aware. I know each and every one of you will be professional. Now, let's get ready." He glanced at his watch. "We've got fourteen minutes until the marshals will deliver the patient to the landing pad."

"C'mon," Lin said to Eva. "I'll show you where all of the medical equipment is stored."

"Hey, Eva," Brett called out.

She turned. "Yeah?"

He touched his chest. "Your lanyard," he said. "You can't wear it. It's a safety hazard. The cards can catch the light. And the cord can wrap around your neck."

"Oh." Eva pulled the ID over her head. Winding the cord around her hand, she shoved the whole thing into her breast pocket. "Thanks."

"No problem," he said.

He watched her walk away. Just like he'd noticed before, the flight suit hugged her curves and accentuated her round ass. Brett's mouth went dry.

"Weird that she's on our crew," said Wade, his voice not much more than a whisper.

"I was surprised to see her, that's for sure."

"And you aren't going to tell me what happened between you two?"

Clapping his hand on the taller man's shoulder, Brett said, "She's part of my flight crew. Anything I say about her now will get me an unpleasant meeting with Darla in HR. Nobody wants that."

"Looks like you lucked out, then," said Wade. "I won't bring it up again."

"I'm glad that at least one thing has gone my way today," he said. "Now, let's hope that nothing goes wrong with our infamous patient."

Eva pressed stethoscope to the patient's chest and listened to his respiration. For now, Decker was asleep, resting from the pain meds he'd been given prior to take-off. Both of his wrists were handcuffed to the gurney he lay on.

She'd heard all the news reports about the serial killer who'd been on the run for more than a year. His story was personally important to her because the communities he'd terrorized—Encantador and the neighboring town of Mercy—were where she'd grown up. But it was more than that.

Decker had killed her grandmother's neighbor.

Then, he'd kidnapped another person from the same housing development.

Decker had killed several people, including a podcaster from San Antonio, before being caught by the undersheriff in Encantador. During his capture, the patient had been beaten, shot and burned. But the wounds had healed enough that he no longer needed acute care. Which, she supposed, was why he was going to be sent to regional jail to await trial.

She pulled the earpieces free before replacing her headset. As she tucked the stethoscope into a pouch that hung from a hook on the fuselage, she figured that her current patient was probably one of the reasons her grandmother had fallen.

Only a few weeks before, Decker had killed one of Baba's neighbors, a woman named Connie Wray. He'd recorded the killing and then sent the video to everyone in Connie's contact list. Getting that message had devastated her grandmother. In fact, after it happened, Eva had taken a week off to stay with Baba. It was one of the reasons she couldn't ask for more time off now. But she imagined that even with Decker in custody, her grandmother was still under some serious stress. Who wouldn't be? She'd lost a neighbor and a friend in such a violent way.

"What's the verdict?" The US marshal spoke into the mic that was attached to his headset. Augustin Herrera wore a black windbreaker with the marshal's seal embroidered on the chest. He was in his fifties, with dark eyes and a sprinkling of gray in his otherwise black crew cut. He had a close-cropped beard and wore a gold crucifix on a gold chain.

"His pulse and respiration are all normal," said Eva. Even with ear protection, the constant *whomp-whomp-whomp* of the rotors drowned out most other sounds.

"How long will this trip take us?" Augustin yelled into his mic.

It was Brett who answered. "Now that we're out of San Antonio, it's about one hundred and twenty miles to Encantador. The flight should only last us half an hour. Forty minutes, tops."

Below the helicopter, San Antonio's downtown, a sea of glass and pavement, had been replaced by the suburbs. Neat houses had been built one next to each other until the properties looked like a quilt from ten thousand feet in the air.

While speaking to the marshal, Brett had turned to look over his seat in the cockpit. In his flight helmet, headset and sunglasses, he looked like the quintessential pilot. Competent. Fearless. Handsome.

Eva turned to Decker once more. True, she'd seen pictures of the killer—had even watched a documentary on his crimes while texting Katya. In those portraits, Decker looked terrifying. A slight man with blue eyes so icy she felt cold just watching the show. But cuffed to the bed and asleep, he didn't seem threatening at all. Still, she knew enough to be wary.

Stacy sat in the cockpit next to Brett. Situated directly behind the cockpit was the cargo hold, which made up much of the aircraft. It was not a big space, but had enough room for transporting a patient, equipment, and medical personnel. Lin and Wade were buckled into seats on the opposite side of the hold. A jump seat, bolted to the fuselage, sat next to the stretcher. Typically, Eva would have occupied that seat. But for now, Augustin sat next to his prisoner.

There was medical equipment for any kind of trauma or emergency. The jaws of life, its handle clamped shut, hung from the wall. There was also equipment to deliver a baby, Narcan for those who'd overdosed, medications, sutures, gauze, bandages and an AED for anyone in cardiac arrest. The medevac was better stocked than most ambulances, and she was glad to see that she had everything she might need. After all, once they dropped off the patient, she still had several more hours left in her shift and would likely be called out on other medical emergencies.

Stacy's voice came in over the mic. "Where'd that come from?"

Eva glanced out the starboard window at the darkening sky. She'd been so focused on the patient and equipment that she hadn't paid attention to anything beyond her patient.

Brett cursed. "I thought we had clear weather the whole way."

"We did," said Stacy, a note of panic in her voice. "The storm came out of nowhere."

"We'll be okay," said Brett. Then to the whole crew, he announced, "Everyone strap in and hang on. It's going to get bumpy."

Another jump seat was folded up behind the pilot's seat. Eva didn't want to leave her patient's side. But she wasn't ready to make the marshal move, either. She wrapped her hand into the webbing that held the AED onto the fuselage. She glanced out of the window again. In the distance, dark clouds filled the horizon. A fork of lightning lit up, yellow against the black.

"Brett," she said, feeling some of the same panic as she'd heard in Stacy's voice. How were they supposed to fly through that? "That storm is huge. Can't we go around it?"

"We're too close to alter our course now. Our only other option is to turn around, he said. "But it's moving fast."

"No way are we going back," said Augustin. "This prisoner is supposed to be at a hearing in less than an hour. If we turn around now, we'll never make it."

"But if it's not safe in the air, then none of us will make it to Encantador," said Eva.

Brett turned in his seat, facing the crew. "The front isn't too wide, only a few miles or so. I can make it through, I think."

"You think?" she echoed.

"Brett's a good pilot," said Lin. "He won't fly into anything he can't fly out of."

Before she could say anything, the patient grimaced in his sleep.

"Did you hear that?" Augustin tapped Eva's arm to get her attention. "He said something."

Eva removed her headset and leaned close to the patient. She couldn't hear anything beyond the noise of the rotors. "What'd he say?"

"Dunno." The marshal unbuckled his harness and moved behind her. "Is he okay?"

She slid in next to the patient.

Decker worked his fingers through the sides of the sheet. His eyebrows were drawn together, and he moved his lips.

She removed her headset and bent close, coming nose to nose with a killer. "Mr. Newcombe," she yelled to be heard over the noise. "My name is Eva Tamke. I'm a nurse with San Antonio Med, and right now, you're on a helicopter. We're taking you to a court hearing." She knew that even in his highly medicated state, he might be lucid enough to know that he was somewhere other than the hospital and therefore confused. "Can you hear me, Mr. Newcombe? Are you uncomfortable?"

His lips moved.

To the marshal, she said, "He's speaking but I can't tell what he's trying to say." She leaned closer. Decker's breath was sour and hot on her ear.

"Ana," Decker said. "Why did you go? Was it because of him?"

She stood up and looked at the marshal. "Do you know anyone named Ana?"

He shook his head. "Nobody comes to mind," he yelled. "But I'll tell my supervisors when we land."

That was when the bottom of the world dropped out from beneath Eva. One minute she was standing next to the stretcher. The next, she was lifted from her feet and slammed into the webbing on the ceiling of the chopper. The chopper bucked, buffeted by gusts of wind and troughs of air on all sides. She fell, landing, nose to nose, on top of Decker.

Before she could move, she heard a sharp crack, like a vase being thrown to the floor. The stretcher beneath her began to roll. Her impact had broken the metal clasp that locked the wheels to the floor of the hold.

Decker's eyes opened. They were the same icy blue

she'd seen in all his photographs. "What the hell?" he growled.

The stretcher was still rolling. She couldn't safely jump off. "My name's Eva Tamke. I'm a nurse—"

"I don't care who you are. Get off of me." He thrashed. The cuffs that tethered his wrists to the sides of the stretcher rattled.

The blood in her veins turned icy. It didn't matter that he was handcuffed to the bed. Decker Newcombe was a dangerous and deadly man. She pushed herself back at the same moment as the helicopter lifted. The loose stretcher rolled back, stealing her traction and keeping her on top of the killer.

Decker started to howl. His legs hadn't been shackled, and he kicked. Augustin dove toward the stretcher, hanging on to Decker's feet. It left her with nowhere to go.

Outside, rain washed over the starboard window in a single sheet. A bolt of lightning streaked by. The scent of ozone hung in the air, and still the killer struggled.

Holding on to the stretcher's railing, she launched herself over the side. The helicopter bucked, dropping hundreds of feet in a single second. She was never sure if it was the steep descent or the weight of her body. But as she dropped over the edge, the whole stretcher tipped to its side.

She screamed as Decker, hanging from his wrists, was pinned on top of her.

She could see two pair of feet as the marshal and one of the EMTs tried to heave the gurney up and over. She scooted back, slithering to get out from under the stretcher. A set of hands grabbed her ankles and pulled her free.

"Wade." Her eyes were wet with terror and relief. "Thank you."

He helped her to her feet. "I got you."

Like the crack of a whip, another bolt of lightning struck outside the helicopter. "That's too close for comfort," said Brett. "I'm taking us lower to the ground."

Decker's gurney was still upside down. The patient was still chained to the railing by his arms. He snarled, the sound feral and full of fury.

They had to get him right-side up. "Everyone, grab a side," Eva said.

She gripped the foot of the stretcher. Lin unbuckled himself and took the head. Wade was at the right and Augustin at the left. Everyone grabbed on to the railing.

"One. Two. Lift." Eva crouched down, pushing with her legs and lifting with her back and arms. Her muscles strained with pain and effort. The gurney rose from the floor several inches. The railing bit into her palms, but they couldn't get any more height.

The stretcher—with Decker on it—was too heavy.

He was right. "Everyone, lower the stretcher carefully."

"Don't you put me back down," Decker screamed. "I'll kill all of you mother…" The rest of his curses were lost by a boom of thunder.

Despite his threats, they lowered the gurney to the floor.

The helicopter dropped into a trough of turbulence, and Eva's stomach landed in her shoes. They had to get the patient flipped over. But how? There was barely enough room in the hold for the four passengers.

"How's it going back there?" Brett asked.

"Not good, but we've got it under control," she said.

"I have an idea," Lin said. "What if we wedged something under the right side of the stretcher and then flipped Decker over?"

"Or we can go with the obvious," said Wade. "Unlock the guy from his handcuffs, and then we can maneuver the stretcher no problem."

"I'm not going to unlock those cuffs," Augustin said, pressing his hand to the front pocket of his pants.

The helicopter shuddered as another strike of lightning lit up the sky.

From the copilot's seat, Stacy cursed. "Holy crap. Holy crap. Holy crap!"

"What's going on?" Lin asked.

But Eva already knew. The control panel, which had been illuminated before, was now dark. The steady beating of the rotors had gone silent.

"That last lightning strike fried our electrical system." Brett gritted his teeth. "Everyone, brace yourselves. We're going to crash."

Chapter 6

Brett stared at the blank instrument panel, and his gut turned watery. They'd taken a direct hit from a bolt of lightning. His electrical system was fried.

He pressed his feet onto the torque peddles.

Nothing.

He jerked the stick from side to side. Front to back. He still had some control, but only a fraction of the maneuverability he once had. Thankfully, there had been enough thrust that they were still aloft and moving forward. But the aircraft was losing altitude fast. He didn't know how long inertia would be on their side.

Without his control panel, he had no way to gauge their altitude. Still, they wouldn't stay in the air much longer than a few minutes.

His training would get him through this. He was the pilot. He was in charge. The souls on the aircraft were his responsibility. Since staying in the air wasn't an option, he had to get the helicopter onto the ground as safely as possible.

It was going to be a bumpy landing at best.

And the chaos in the hold was far from optimal.

"Everyone." He had to yell to be heard over the wind

and the storm. "Strap in." Then to Stacy, he said, "Try to contact air traffic control. Let them know that we're going down."

She flipped several switches. "Mayday. Mayday. This is MEDEVAC November-Charlie-Charlie-One-Six-Niner-Two. MEDEVAC November-Charlie-Charlie-One-Six-Niner-Two. We've lost power and are going down." She also gave the last known coordinates. Looking at Brett, she shook her head. "I don't think anyone heard me."

Texas airspace was monitored by a web of radar towers. When the helicopter disappeared, someone would notice. What's more, they'd come looking for the crash site.

"See if you can find a place to land," Brett said.

Stacy turned in her seat, looking out the window. "Down there. At two o'clock," she said.

The storm had turned the sky black. Rain washed over the windshield. Beneath the aircraft were hills, rocks and desert. Then, ahead and to the right, he saw a flat piece of ground. No large boulders. At the edge of the clearing was a dry stream bed and beyond that, a steep hill. If they could make it to the opening, he could do a running landing and put the helicopter down.

It wouldn't be a perfect landing. Certainly, someone would get injured on the way down. Eva's face flashed into his mind. His chest filled with the need to protect her.

He had to focus, or nobody would survive the crash.

Pulling the control stick hard, he focused on the valley below. His arms burned with the effort. His heart slammed against his ribs until his chest ached. His pulse echoed in his skull.

The helicopter pointed its nose a little to the right.

Would it be enough for them to make the clearing?

The ground was coming up fast. A sure sign that they were losing altitude.

He wasn't worried about bringing back an intact helicopter, but he did care about bringing back a whole crew. Brett focused on the piece of ground where he wanted to put his skids in the dirt. It was as if the sheer force of his will could land the helicopter.

He gripped the control stick harder. "C'mon. C'mon," he urged. "Don't you give out on me now."

Beside him, Stacy tried to send out another SOS.

From the back of the helicopter came Wade's panicked voice. "It's all too heavy."

Brett knew that the patient had tipped over in the back of the hold and that the crew had been trying to get the gurney upright. Decker yelled like a wounded beast. Brett didn't have time to worry about the killer. But what would happen to everyone else if the stretcher wasn't secured?

Actually, he knew the answer. With a gurney tumbling around in the hold, it wouldn't matter if everyone was securely buckled into their seats. The outcome wouldn't be pretty.

Before he could say a word. Stacy had unbuckled her harness and backed out of the cockpit. "I'm gonna help them with that stretcher. Back in a sec!"

He was about to yell for her to return and buckle up when a gust of wind hit the chopper from portside. It nudged the aircraft to the right. His nose was facing the clearing, but the ground was coming up too quickly. He wasn't sure how to keep the helicopter aloft in any case. But maybe he'd finally gotten a bit of good luck. Their heading was correct, and their speed had dropped enough for a safe—or safe-ish—landing.

"Stacy," he yelled. "Get back in your seat. Everyone else, buckle up."

There was nothing else to do but pray that they all made it out alive.

"One. More. Second," Stacy groaned. "We've almost got it secured."

They didn't have another second. The skids hit the peak of the hill that ringed the valley. The aircraft staggered to the right, sliding down. A cloud of dirt and mud billowed around them as they hit the bottom of the hill and started to roll. The helicopter was like a pebble that had been thrown into a dryer.

From the back, there was crashing and cursing.

There was the sharp crack of metal snapping in two. The tail rotor cartwheeled away.

Interspersed were memories.

There was the moment he'd gotten the news that he was going from basic training to flight school.

The first time his instructor pilot let him take the controls, and he soared through the air.

Last night, when he'd shown up at the restaurant, a beautiful woman with dark hair and a coral dress smiled at him. She approached with her palm outstretched. "You must be Brett," she said. "I'm Eva."

As she slipped her palm into his, one word filled his mind.

Home.

Brett didn't have time to examine any other memories from his life, both good and bad. He was in the pilot's seat. The helicopter bounced along the ground as if in a drunken frenzy.

Metal tore with a sickening screech. Brett turned in time to see the tail of his helicopter being ripped from the rest of the fuselage. At the back of his aircraft was a gaping mouth with jagged teeth.

Wind and rain blew in through the opening. The stretcher that had caused so much chaos was sucked out and into the storm. It skidded on its side before Brett could see it no more.

Then, the aircraft slowed, finally coming to rest on its side in the dried creek bed. The screaming had stopped, and the silence was more terrifying than the constant noise. At some point, the windshield had shattered and torn away. Rain fell into the cockpit.

Brett's breath came ragged and short. He quickly scanned his body. Every part of him was sore, but nothing pained him. Unfastening his harness, he dropped from the seat and looked into the hold. It was a tangle of wires, metal and metal equipment. There was no movement. No signs of life.

"Hello," he called out.

There was no answer.

The metallic taste of panic coated his tongue. He swallowed it away. He'd been trained to survive a crash. He knew what to do. Brett mentally listed all the tasks he had to complete. Turning back to the control panel, he made sure the engine was off and there was no power to the aircraft. Right now, a fire would be devastating to any survivors. Since the lightning had fried the electrical system, it was easy work.

Now, he had to find and give aid to the survivors. All the souls on this chopper were his responsibility. Moving from the chair, he stood in the small space between the pilot and copilot's seats. He called out again. "Hello?"

Nothing.

He took one step into the hold.

Stacy's body was sprawled out near the cockpit. There was a long gash across her neck. She stared at nothing. Without question, she was dead. He closed his eyes for a second at the horror. The side of her helmet was crushed. The visor was broken. Blood soaked her flight suit, turning the fabric black. He knew the awful truth but grabbed her wrist anyway. There was no pulse. Her skin had already started to cool. He reached under her chin, searching for a pulse on her throat.

Nothing more could be done. He gently ran a hand over her face, closing her eyes. Then he turned to look at the rest of the wreckage.

The hold of his aircraft was strewn with medical equipment. Cargo netting from the ceiling dangled down. Wires, ripped from the walls, hung freely. The stench of fuel filled the air, burning his throat and eyes. Thank goodness there was no power. A single spark would've ignited the fumes.

His jaw was tight. There had been seven souls on the helicopter, himself included. He had to account for them all. Yet he couldn't help but wonder about one person in particular.

Where was Eva?

* * *

Decker's left shoulder hurt like hell. His head pounded, like someone had turned his skull into a snare drum. His whole body ached, and he was somehow cold and wet. When was Nurse Nancy with the salty sense of humor going to show up with the, as she called them, fun meds?

Like the sun breaking over the horizon, the reality of the situation dawned on him. He'd been in the back of a helicopter. But why?

Oh, now he remembered. There'd been a brunette. She'd told him her name was Eva, and she was also a nurse. He was being taken to Encantador for a court hearing. And then? Well, Nurse Eva hadn't said. But Decker knew that during the hearing, he'd be charged with all his crimes and thrown into jail.

There had been a storm. Turbulence. Lightning. The chopper had gone down.

And now what?

He looked up. Rain fell, pelting him in the face. He was still cuffed to the stretcher by one arm. The other arm? Well, that was an entirely different matter. The railing had broken, and he now just had the bracelet attached to his wrist. He could live with that.

His legs were free.

Flipping around, he kicked the railing. Once. Twice. The effort left him winded. He hadn't been out of bed much in days and days. His muscles were weak. The headache had gone from feeling like he was a drum set in a garage band to becoming the target in bazooka practice.

It was all the damn meds he'd been given in the hospital. Nurse Nancy had turned him into a cracked-out junkie.

Lying on his back, he gulped in air and rainwater.

The water cooled and refreshed him, and then he turned cold. Clad only in a hospital gown, Decker had on a single sock with treads on both the top and bottom. He didn't know where the other sock was now.

Turning so his feet touched the railing, he pressed with all his strength. There was a snap of metal, and then the weight of the railing pulled his arm to the ground.

His little-used muscles strained as he struggled to sit up. Leaning on the stretcher, he breathed. After a moment, he pulled his arm, still cuffed to a section of railing, to his lap. A spindly slat connected the upper piece with the bottom. Given time and something heavy, he could break the plastic and metal. But for now, he had neither.

He swayed as he stood. His vision grew foggy around the edges, but Decker refused to pass out. A moment later, his wooziness passed, and he surveyed his surroundings.

He was in the middle of a clearing, with hills on all sides. The rain had turned the hard-packed ground to silty mud. The helicopter's rotor and tail were both more than twenty yards to his left. To his right was the rest of the aircraft.

Honestly, Decker didn't like being stranded with no food, no water, no clothes and no idea where he really was. But he did have one thing that he hadn't had in a while. His freedom.

Still, the wrecked chopper was sure to bring a search

party. If Decker wanted to stay free, then he had to be gone before anyone showed up.

Placing one foot before the other, he staggered toward the rear section of the broken fuselage. Once he reached the broken rotor, he could see the trench dug in the ground by the helicopter as it skidded over the ground. He started to walk the perimeter. There had to be something he could use to break the railing.

It was then that Decker saw him.

At first, Decker assumed that the lump was another rock. But it moved. Moaned. Once he started paying attention, he could hear the wheezing breath.

He walked to where the person lay on the ground.

It was a marshal. He'd have pegged the guy for law enforcement even if the dude wasn't wearing a windbreaker with the US Marshal seal embroidered on the chest.

The man's nose was bloody and misshapen. His leg bent at an unnatural angle, undoubtedly broken. With the rain, it was hard to tell what was blood and what was soil.

The man met Decker's gaze. His eyes were wide, filled with equal measures of terror and rage. "You," he panted.

Holding the piece of railing in one hand, Decker lifted his other hand. The broken chain hung from the cuff. "I assume you have keys for this. Why don't you hand them over, and I'll make it easy for you?"

"I'm not giving you shit," the marshal said. Blood mixed with his spittle.

"You can give the keys to me nice-like. Or I'm going

to take them, and I won't be gentle." Maybe all the things that people wrote and said about Decker was right. He might be a twisted son of a bitch. Because, honestly, he loved messing with this guy. It wasn't just that the man, who was seriously injured, was trying to be feisty. It was that Decker had all the power. They both knew it.

"No." The man spit on the ground. Bloody foam clung to his lips.

"Give me the goddamn key."

"Okay. Okay." The marshal held up one hand in surrender. With his other hand he slowly pulled down the windbreaker's zipper. "They're inside my jacket."

"Go ahead." Decker was ready for anything.

When the man brandished a gun, he wasn't surprised. Without thought, he swung the railing. It caught the marshal's wrist. There was a crack, a scream, and the firearm flew from the man's hand. Decker couldn't see where it landed.

"Jesus, that hurts." The marshal cradled his wrist.

"You done being cute?"

"You broke my wrist."

"You pointed a gun at me. So I don't know why you're whining. You and I both know that you're about to die."

"Wait. Let me tell you something about me."

Decker had seen this all before, when the doomed tried to tell him about their lives and tap into his humanity. He'd lost every shred of compassion long ago.

"I have two children," the marshal said in a pleading voice. "Auggie Junior. We call him AJ. He's eleven years old. My daughter Gabriella is fifteen. They need me."

Eleven years old. Like Decker's own kid—if the

hacker was right. Not for the first time, he wondered about his boy. Was he tall for his age? Or smart? Or kind? In short, was the kid all the things that Decker was not?

"Well, Marshal," Decker said, straddling the man's chest. "I'll tell you what *I* need—those keys."

Holding the railing in both hands, he shoved the end onto the man's neck.

The marshal didn't struggle long. There was no real satisfaction in killing a dying man. But as the marshal breathed his last, Decker felt the power of life over death. He knew he was invincible.

Once the man was gone, Decker patted him down. Funny thing, the marshal hadn't lied entirely. A set of handcuff keys were tucked into the pocket of his pants. Decker worked the key into the lock, springing the bracelets on both hands loose. He rolled his wrists and looked down at the dead man.

There was more that the marshal could provide Decker knelt, his knees popping. Lifting the man's foot, he checked the sole of his cowboy boot. Size eleven, only half a size bigger than Decker. Close enough.

He pulled one boot off and then the other. Decker grabbed the man's socks and worked his jeans off, leaving the belt in the loops. He eyed the dead guy for what else he could take. Decker wasn't above much, but he drew the line at used skivvies. He stripped out of his hospital garb. Shivering and naked, he rubbed rainwater over his skin. Then he pulled on the jeans. They were too big around the waist and too long. He folded the cuff and tightened his belt.

In the back pocket was a thick wallet. He kept the cash. He threw a stack of business cards, credit cards and a set of family photos onto the ground.

Next, he stripped off the jacket. It was warm and waterproof—two things Decker needed most.

In the pockets, he found three dollars in change and a cell phone. He threw the phone onto the ground next to the pictures. Getting rid of the device pained him, but he figured it was a work phone. Surely the marshals had installed some kind of tracking device.

Decker worked his feet into the socks and boots. It gave him a moment to think about the crash. The aircraft had somersaulted like a drunken monkey across the valley. He remembered the screeching of metal as the tail section was ripped free and the gust of wind that sucked him out of the jagged hole. There was no way anyone could've survived. It meant he was on his own.

Just like his grandsire, Jack the Ripper. All those years ago, when his ancestor had stalked the streets of Whitechapel, had he encountered setbacks?

After all, there was the story of the third victim. A woman's body had been found in the courtyard of a tavern. The man who found her had mistaken the corpse for the prone body of his inebriated wife. He'd gone inside the establishment for help, but not before his horse was spooked by something.

In the dark, it was impossible to tell if someone else had been in the courtyard that night. Hiding.

Had Jack the Ripper almost been caught?

Slipping into his jacket, Decker knew that the need to kill was part of his DNA. But there was also the need to survive and the ability to outwit law enforcement that had come down through the generations, as well. Until recently, Decker hadn't thought much about his own legacy, other than what the history books would recall of the terror he caused. But now, he knew that he had a son.

Had the kid inherited anything of Decker?

Did the need to kill run in his blood, as well?

After finding the marshal's gun, he began to walk.

There was only one place for him to go. He had to get to Mexico and get the phone that he'd stashed. It was the only way to reach Seraphim.

He had to know more about Ana. Because if she'd given birth to Decker's child and never told him about the kid, then he was going to make her pay.

Chapter 7

Eva sucked in a breath. Her chest burned, and the stench of gasoline hung in the air. She lay on the floor of the helicopter's hold. They'd been trying to secure the stretcher when the aircraft went down. Nobody had been buckled into their seats, hoping they had a few precious seconds to complete their task. Honestly, she didn't know how she'd survived the impact.

Yet she remembered it all.

There was the weightless moment when the chopper dropped out of the sky. Then the thundering as they skidded across the ground. Her head throbbed, and her ears were filled with the sound of a million angry bees.

Around the buzzing, she heard Brett's voice. "Eva. Can you hear me? Are you okay?"

She pried her eyelids apart. Everything in her vision wavered, surrounded by a haze. Blinking hard, she opened her eyes again.

He knelt in front of her. Worry lines creased his brow.

"Brett," she croaked. Her throat was so dry. She coughed and swallowed. The taste of fuel clung to her lips. "How is everyone?"

He pressed his lips together so hard they turned white. *1*

Giving a single shake of his head, he said, "Not good. In fact, everyone's…" He worked his jaw back and forth. "The whole crew is dead."

"All of them?" She didn't know Lin or Stacy well at all, but Wade had been a friend. They were on the same team that played trivia at a local bar every Wednesday night. He was quick with an answer and quicker still with a joke or a laugh. She always enjoyed his company and couldn't believe that the lively EMT was gone. For a moment, she couldn't breathe. "Are you sure?"

"Positive," he said. "I checked everyone's pulse."

But there had been more than the crew on the helicopter. "What about the marshal? The patient?"

Brett looked toward the rear of the helicopter. She followed his gaze. The rear section of the aircraft had been pulled off. "I haven't found them yet," he said, his voice hollow.

Brett said he'd checked for a pulse. But what if it was there, and he'd missed the signs of life? After all, he was a pilot. She was the nurse. She had to check the rest of the crew herself. Besides, Augustin Herrera and Decker Newcombe were both out there somewhere. They might be alive and need medical care.

Pushing against the floor, she tried to sit up.

Brett placed a strong hand on her shoulder, holding her in place. "Just rest a minute. We need to make sure you aren't hurt."

If Eva were a patient at SAMC, then she would be given several scans—an X-ray, an MRI and a CAT scan at least. Right now, she didn't have the luxury of so-phisticated medical equipment, and there were no acute pains. While that didn't necessarily mean she wasn't injured, it was a good sign.

She held out her hand to Brett. "Help me up. I want to recheck the rest of the crew, and if there's nothing to be done…"

"There isn't," he interrupted.

She ignored him and continued, "We'll gather some medical equipment and see if we can find the marshal and his prisoner."

Brett placed his palm in hers. His hand was strong, firm and, somehow, reassuring. A flash of memory came to her. They were standing in his kitchen, and he'd reached for her hand. In that moment, she'd felt such a strong rush of desire that his touch left her breathless. Even now, with her hand in his, her pulse raced. She wanted to ignore her reaction, but it was unmistakable.

He pulled, and she rose to her feet. After standing, she placed all her weight on her feet. A sharp pain shot through her leg. She gritted her teeth.

"What's the matter?" Brett held her hand tighter. "Does something hurt?"

Honestly, everything on her body ached. "It's my left leg."

He knelt in front of her. "Can I look at it?"

"Sure," she said.

Brett gently pulled up the leg of her flight suit.

Last night, he'd knelt in front of her for an entirely different reason. To her, it seemed like their tryst never actually happened. Maybe it was all an erotic fever dream. But still, his touch was familiar and all too real.

"Ouch," he said, prodding her shin. "You've got a

heck of a bruise. I can't tell if you broke anything or not, though. Can you stand on it?"

The old test of broken bones not being able to bear any weight wasn't an exact science. Many people had multiple breaks and could move the appendage. Still, she shifted her weight to her left foot. Eva couldn't help herself. She cursed, and tears collected at the corner of her eyes.

"It's okay," said Brett, his voice as soothing as his hand had been reassuring. "I know we've got an air cast around here somewhere. It won't be perfect, especially if you've broken something. But it'll be better than agony." He held out a strip of cargo netting. "Hold on to this."

She wrapped her wrist through the webbing and let her arm bear much of her weight. It was then that she looked around the helicopter.

Wade lay several yards away. His eyes were open, yet he stared at nothing. His gaze was already turning milky. Lin was next to him. His eyes were closed, but a pool of blood so dark red it looked like tar surrounded him. Even from where she stood, she could tell that he no longer drew breath.

Turned out that Brett was right. Everyone on the crew was dead.

As an ER nurse, she'd faced death more than once. But never had it been this personal—this close to her. How was it that the Grim Reaper had come for Lin and Wade and Stacy but ignored her? And what were the chances that the US marshal or the killer had survived being sucked out of the helicopter's rear?

She knew the answer to the last question.

The odds of either man being alive was low.

Grief and guilt hit her with a double punch, and she saw stars.

Brett dug through the debris of the crash. He held up a preformed plastic boot with straps. "Found it. I can get it on you if you want."

"Thanks." She held tighter to the strap and lifted her foot. It took Brett only a few minutes to remove her sneaker and put the boot on her foot. He tightened the strap, and the throbbing eased to a dull ache. Setting her foot down, she sighed. "That's better."

"Glad I could help."

Help. The word resonated through her chest. "How are we supposed to get out of here? Does anyone know where we are?" She paused and drew in a breath. "Do we even know where we are?"

"Best I can tell, we're north of Encantador by about sixty miles. The interstate is that way." He pointed toward the cockpit. Stacy was on the floor. Her flight suit was stained with blood. "It's about twenty miles from here."

Eva had driven that same stretch of highway more times than she could remember. It was the artery that connected her hometown with San Antonio. But really, it was a narrow lane that ran through the middle of a vast desert. Even if they headed in the right direction, what were the chances of them finding the road? Not good. "What about making a call? Or is there a beacon onboard?"

"I checked my phone. No bars," he said. "What about you?"

Eva's phone was tucked into one of the many pockets on her flight suit. She removed the device. The ceramic shield was shattered. The screen had turned an eerie shade of green, and it flickered. She held up the device for Brett to see. "My phone's pretty much trashed."

"Even if we can't make a call, the FAA will notice that we went down. They'll have a reasonable idea of where we are and come looking. On top of that, there's an emergency beacon that will send out a ping with our location. So long as we stay close to the aircraft, they'll find us in a day or two."

"A day or two?" she echoed. But really, it wasn't that bad. She knew that it was protocol to stock the air ambulance with water, emergency rations, medical equipment, blankets. If it turned out that they were stranded for a few days, they'd survive.

She looked around at the carnage. "Let's gather up all the food and water. We need the med kit." A large plastic case, like a jumbo tackle box, was hanging on the wall. It was white with a red cross painted on the top and sides and had a red plastic handle. She pulled it free. "Where are the blankets stored?"

"We'll get those in a minute," said Brett. He held a box of food, wrapped in plastic, atop a case of water. "Let's pile everything outside. I'm not spooked or anything, but I'd like to set up camp away from the bodies."

The corpses were another problem. Too soon the scent of blood would attract wild animals. "We'll have to do something with them, you know," she said. "We can't just leave them in the helicopter to rot."

"I know," he said. "I just haven't figured out what's

best." Even though there was a gaping hole at the back of the helicopter, Brett jiggled the lever handle for the service door. It didn't budge. He slammed his palm against the hull. "Dammit."

The aircraft rocked, and Eva froze. Sure, Brett had hit the wall. But it had been a slap of frustration. He definitely hadn't used enough force to move an entire helicopter. In the distance, she could hear the chug of an approaching locomotive. "Is that a train?"

"It can't be," said Brett. "There's no track around for miles."

She had grown up in the area and knew he was right. And yet. "What's that sound?"

He stood still. "I don't hear anything."

"You don't?" Maybe she had a concussion and was having auditory hallucinations. She went still and listened again. The sound was still there. "That. Do you hear that? It sounds like an engine."

"Maybe," said Brett. "Yeah, I hear it now."

The helicopter shimmied, and she looked out the window. Her blood turned icy in her veins. A wall of mud, water and debris filled the creek bed and was headed straight for them.

"Run!" she shouted, pushing Brett away from the door.

They moved through the back of the helicopter, both of them slowed by what they carried—Brett the food and water, and Eva the med kit. Her injury and boot didn't help, either.

The hull vibrated with the oncoming flash flood. She

could smell the debris, earthy and rotten, as it rolled forward.

In the boot, she was too slow.

"Get out of here." She refused to let Brett die on her account. And for a single moment, she was glad that her last night was spent in his arms. "Go without me." The words tasted sour.

"That's not going to happen." His eyes blazed. He dropped the cases of food and water and lifted her from the ground. "Wrap your arms around my neck and don't let go. We are both getting out of here alive."

She held on to his neck, trying not to let the med kit bang against his back. As Brett picked his way out of the helicopter. She glanced once at the approaching water as he sprinted up the bank. The stream filled as she crawled the final feet. Lying on the muddy ground, she stared as roiling black water rushed past.

She rolled onto her back and clutched the med kit to her chest. The storm wasn't done with them yet. Rain still fell, dampening her hair and pooling on her flight suit.

There was a screech of metal being torn from metal. She sat up and watched the water push the chopper downstream, taking with it the bodies of the dead crew. And the homing beacon, as well. When the authorities zeroed in on a location, it would be miles from the actual crash site.

Eva surveyed her surroundings. They truly were in the middle of nowhere. She looked at Brett. He was lying on the ground, chest heaving with each breath. She had the strongest urge to rest her head on his shoulder and let him rub her back. He'd done as much the night before, right after they'd made love for the second—or was it the third?—time.

"Thanks for saving me," she said.

"I wasn't going to leave you."

"What now?" she asked.

"I say we climb to the top of that ridge." He pointed to a set of hills. "See if we can pick up a cell signal."

In the distance, she could see the helicopter's tail. But there was more. She wiped the rain from her face and looked again. She could see a wheel and a metal bar.

"Is that the stretcher?"

"I think so," said Brett.

She held up the plastic box with a bright red cross. "Thank goodness I didn't lose this."

"Agreed." Holding out his hand, he offered, "I can carry it."

For a moment, she thought about declining. After all, she was a grown woman and didn't need a man's help to survive. But this was different. If she truly wanted to make it out of this situation alive, she was going to need Brett. Finally, she handed him the pack. His fingers grazed the back of her hand.

After everything, she didn't expect a current of electricity to buzz up her arm. But it did. "Thanks," she said.

She couldn't be distracted by her libido.

Too much was at stake.

"Let's see if there's something in here for you to take," he said.

Honestly, Eve wasn't worried about herself. If that was the stretcher in the distance, a few seconds could be the difference between life and death for the patient. "We should go," she said. "I need to check and see if anyone else survived."

Brett had already taken a knee and opened the med kit. He rooted around, shifting the contents. It gave her a moment to study him, even though she wanted to sprint to the stretcher. Yet, he was right. She wasn't getting far with her foot the way it was.

His shoulders were broad. His chin was well defined. He still had a small bruise where she'd bitten the side of his neck the night before. Her body heated at the memory.

But there was more to Brett than just his good looks or that fact that he was excellent in bed. Last night, she'd found him to be charming and funny. But today, she'd seen him in a crisis and knew he was so much more. He was a good leader. Competent. Caring. He'd risked his own life to save hers.

Eva had learned early on that relying too much on others was a sure way to be disappointed. But she had no choice other than to work with Brett.

That meant she had to keep her emotions in check.

Brett stood, holding up a packet filled with OTC pain meds. "This should help."

She took the packet, careful not to touch his hand. Eva didn't want to get distracted by that connection between them again. "Thanks."

As they walked, she ripped open a corner and popped the pills into her mouth. She swallowed them without water as best she could.

They continued to walk. The boot was heavy, but it

stabilized her foot and the pain was gone. From several yards away, she could see the back of the stretcher. It lay on its side. The corner of a sheet flapped in the wind. The gurney was surprisingly intact, at least from the back. The only real damage she could see was a broken railing. She couldn't see the patient from where she stood. She wasn't sure if Decker was unconscious or if he'd died in the crash.

The rain had lessened to a drizzle. She wiped her wet hair from her face and approached the stretcher. "Mr. Newcombe." Her voice filled the vast emptiness. "It's Eva, the flight nurse. I'm here to help you." She rounded to the front side of the stretcher.

It was empty.

Had Decker been thrown from the stretcher on impact? It seemed so. But where was his body now?

She scanned the clearing. A dark mass lay on the ground. Even from where she stood, she could tell it was a person. She grabbed Brett's wrist. "See that?"

He followed her gaze. "It's the marshal."

He sprinted to the body. Eva hobbled after him. From a few paces away, she slowed. The missing railing lay next to his body.

Brett knelt next to Augustin and set the med kit on the ground beside him. He placed two fingers under the man's chin, then looked up at Eva, and she knew. Still, Brett shook his head and said, "He's dead."

They were the only survivors of the crash. Completely alone in the wilderness. Aside from the dangers of exposure, there were wild animals to contend with. Her gut clenched around a hard knot of grief and fear.

But there was more.

Augustin Herrera was clad only in his boxers and shirt.

"I don't think Decker got thrown off at all." With the toe of his boot, Brett nudged the railing lying next to the marshal. "That didn't just come loose. The handcuff has been unlocked."

Eva knelt next to Brett and stared at the body. There was bruising on the neck. "His windpipe has been crushed," she said. She'd seen similar injuries while working in the ER. "He was killed."

Her mouth was dry, and her palms turned clammy. She and Brett weren't just stranded and alone in the Texas desert. There was serial killer on the loose. She turned in a slow circle. Hills surrounded the clearing in which they stood. There was nothing else to see, other than thick clouds and dirt, turned to black silt by the recent rain. Yet, she knew that Decker had to be nearby. Was he watching them, even now?

She glanced at the marshal. Was her fate going to be the same?

No. She refused to become Decker's next victim. Between her and Brett, they had years of military service, training and skill sets that could get them out of here alive.

It was ironic. This morning, she'd tried to sneak out of his house. This afternoon, she'd thought about turning down an assignment because it meant working with her one-night stand. Now that they were stranded together, she was grateful he was the man she was trapped with.

Chapter 8

SSA Jason Jones sat in his office in the FBI's building in downtown San Antonio. More than three hundred agents and support staff worked in a high rise located two blocks from the federal courthouse. Jason had a corner office on the seventeenth floor. The wall of windows gave him a view of the San Antonio River along with the restaurants and shops that made up the River Walk.

A computer sat on his desk, its screen filled with a report filed by one of his agents. The 302 outlined how a drug cartel was buying stolen weapons from a street gang. He'd have to meet with his counterparts at the ATF and DEA, but for now, he couldn't concentrate. He jiggled the mouse. The time appeared in the lower corner of his screen: 3:34 p.m.

"Dammit," he cursed quietly. He should have heard something by now.

He picked up the phone on the edge of his desk. The line went directly to his assistant. "Luke, I need you to check on something for me. Find out the status of the medevac flight with Decker Newcombe."

"I'm on it," Luke replied.

Jason turned his seat so he could gaze out the windows. For a moment, he watched people on the street below, but he didn't really see anything. Honestly, until Decker had been arraigned, charged with his crimes and finally sent to jail to wait for his trial, he wouldn't be happy.

Hell, he wouldn't be truly happy until the killer had been found guilty in court.

He was the one who had signed off on the plan for the killer to be flown by air ambulance to Encantador, but he also knew that no plan was foolproof—especially where Decker Newcombe was involved.

Jason stared out the window and watched as tourists wandered on the streets below.

At a sharp knock on his office door, he swiveled to face his desk. "Yeah?"

His assistant stepped inside. Luke was a bright kid with loads of ambition and one day wanted to be an FBI agent. In short, Luke reminded Jason of a younger version of himself. A recent graduate of Texas Midland State University, Luke had been a summer intern while in college. So, when the assistant position became available, Jason offered him the job. After amassing three years of work experience, Luke could apply to become an agent. At that time, he'd put in a good word for the young man. Until then, there was work to be done.

"What have you got for me?"

"It's not good, sir." There was an uncharacteristic break in his voice. He held his phone to his chest, like it was a special toy and would give him courage. For the first time, he looked younger than his twenty-two years. Which was fine, because Jason felt older than dirt. "I spoke to the people at San Antonio Med. They lost contact with the helicopter. It hasn't landed at the hospital in Encantador, either. I put a call into the Texas Aviation Division. They don't have much of anything for me."

Jason's head throbbed. "Except what?"

"Except, there was a pop-up storm that showed up on the route in their flight plan. They're trying to find out if the helicopter is still in the air."

Jason struggled to process all the information. He supposed that was why his first question wasn't the best. "Pop-up storm. That sounds made up. What is that?"

"Well." Luke swallowed. "Usually, storms are caused by a cold or warm front moving into an area. That's what's called a trigger. With a pop-up storm, there is no easily identifiable trigger. But they're not uncommon on hot and humid days. Or at least that's what the lady with the aviation division said."

With a wave of his hand, Jason cleared away all the information. "You know what, forget I asked." He needed to organize his thoughts. One worry was at the top of his mind. What if Decker had gotten away?

Luke's phone began to ring. He glanced at the screen. "It's the aviation division."

"Put it on speaker."

"This is Luke," he said after swiping the call open. "And I've got you on speaker. My boss, Supervisory Special Agent Jason Jones can also hear you." He set the phone on the desk.

"My name is Lola Sanchez. I'm one of the aviation officers for the state. I checked on the air ambulance from

SAMC. We've lost contact. I have the coordinates where the helicopter was last located by our radar."

Jason typed them into his computer as she spoke. A map of southern Texas appeared, along with a red dot sixty miles north of Encantador.

"I've contacted the FAA," Lola continued, "and they're trying to find the tracking device on the aircraft's black box. Right now, I'm sending out a search party. I'll contact you when I hear something."

He was glad that everyone was taking the missing helicopter seriously. But he wasn't about to be left out of the investigation. Besides, he had to be transparent about the situation. "Ms. Sanchez," he began.

"Call me Lola."

"Lola," he said. "There are some things you need to know about that flight. There was one patient onboard being taken to Encantador for arraignment."

"I know," she said. "I saw the flight plan."

"The patient was Decker Newcombe. Which is why we have to be vigilant."

"Understood. What should I tell my search-and-rescue team?" she asked. "They aren't law enforcement."

She was right. Jason didn't know what they would find once they got into the desert. But in his gut, he knew it wasn't going to be good.

A plan came to him, fully formed. He rose from his seat. "I'm on my way to Encantador now. But it will take me a few hours to get onto the scene. The first thing I'm going to do is get in touch with the US Marshals. One of their people was on that aircraft." He pointed at Luke.

The younger man nodded. "Then, I'm going to call in an agency who works in that area."

He opened his desk drawer and removed a shoulder holster and his service firearm, a standard issue SIG Saur. He slipped his arm into the holster and tightened the strap. The gun was heavy, cold and felt like death. He pulled his suit jacket off the back of his chair and slipped it on over his sidearm.

"What agency is that?" Lola asked.

"Tell me," Jason began, "are you familiar with a private security agency called Texas Law?"

Ryan Steele, an operative with Texas Law, sat in his office, a renovated motel outside of Mercy, Texas. There wasn't much to Mercy. Aside from the long strip of reconfigured offices, the Center for Rural Law Enforcement shared a parking lot. Across the road was a gas station with a small restaurant, and next door to that was the post office.

Leaning back in his chair, he knew that he'd been fortunate to get a second chance at life. At one time, he'd been wanted by the police. If he were being honest, he should really be in jail. But he'd made a deal, gone straight, and now he was working a legit job. He was also in love with the local undersheriff, Kathryn Glass.

Who'd have ever thought that of all people, he'd end up in a relationship with a cop?

The man who'd offered Ryan the deal and was now his boss sat on the other side of the desk. Isaac Patton had founded Texas Law a few years before. The agency's first task had been to find the elusive killer Decker Newcombe.

Back in the day, he had acted as Decker's business manager when the man was just a paid assassin. Funny to think about how murder for hire seemed like an easy way to make cash.

But they'd been contacted by a motorcycle club, The Transgressors. They'd wanted Decker to kill a district attorney in the small Wyoming town of Pleasant Pines. There had been other deaths—a security guard and Decker's accomplice—and the murder had been captured on CCTV.

Decker and Ryan had both been wanted men. While Decker disappeared into Mexico, Ryan had been arrested. It was then that Isaac offered him a chance at redemption. In exchange for allowing himself to be the bait that would draw Decker out of hiding, Ryan was promised that his record would be cleared.

It had been several long years with Decker on the run. But finally, the killer had been captured. The wheels of justice were already turning. Soon enough, Decker would be rotting in a small concrete jail cell.

In fact, the hearing to formally charge Decker with multiple murders was the whole reason that Isaac sat on the opposite side of the desk. He wanted to be in the courtroom when the killer was taken away.

The desk phone rang.

"Hopefully," said Isaac, "that's the call we've been waiting for."

Ryan rather expected the caller to be the love of his life, Kathryn, with word that the helicopter had landed at the hospital. But he was at work, and his boss was within easy earshot. He had to be professional. "Hello," he said, answering the phone. "You've reached Texas Law, this is Ryan."

"It's Jason."

"Jason," Ryan repeated. "I've got Isaac with me. We're just waiting for word from the heliport in Encantador."

Kathryn and the sheriff, Maurice "Mooky" Parsons, were waiting at the hospital. As soon as Decker was off the aircraft, they were going to personally escort the killer to the courthouse. Once he'd been charged, Decker would be turned over to the Texas Department of Corrections, where he'd be housed in jail while waiting for his trial.

"I'm glad that Isaac's with you," said the fed. "Can you put the call on speaker? There have been some developments."

A hard knot lodged in the middle of Ryan's throat. Between Jason's tone and his cryptic words, he knew something was up. He swallowed before saying, "Sure thing."

He activated the speaker function and set the handset back onto the cradle. "Jason, you've got both of us now. What's going on?"

"The helicopter's incommunicado. The hospital can't raise it via radio. The FAA can't find it on radar. They flew into a pop-up storm, which apparently is a real thing, and lost contact somewhere about sixty miles north of you. We've reached out to the Marshals Service to get the contact information for their person onboard. But we're still waiting."

"What can we do?" Isaac asked.

"I've got the last known position of the helicopter." Jason read off the coordinates. "It's in the middle of nowhere, but I'd like you to take a team and investigate." He paused and drew in a breath. "Hopefully, it's just a fluke because of the storm. But until we hear from the helicopter, we're all in the dark."

Ryan knew that Jason was wasting energy with hope. If Decker Newcombe was involved, they were only going to find chaos and destruction.

Brett's chest ached. It was like the loss of each of his crew members—each of his friends—was a blade to the heart. But he couldn't give in to grief. He had to formulate a plan. Eva was relying on him. And though no one might know it yet, so was all of Texas law enforcement and the people in this community. A serial killer—with a gun and who knows what else the marshal had had on him—was on the loose.

Eva gestured toward the creek. "Without the helicopter, there's no homing beacon. How's anyone supposed to find us now?" Her voice held an edge of panic.

He hated to leave the crash site, although Eva was right. Without the beacon, the authorities might not even know where to look for survivors. Since he'd dropped the food and water to carry her out of the wreckage, they weren't prepared to wait for a rescue. But to save her life, he'd do it all again.

"Our best plan is to get to the top of that." He pointed toward one of the hills that ringed the small valley. "It's the best chance we have to pick up a cell phone signal."

"What about him?" She pointed to the body of the US marshal. "We can't just leave him here."

Brett hated the idea of *burning daylight*, as his old flight instructor used to say. Especially since in this case they were actually using time that could be spent finding a cell signal. But it was also true that they couldn't leave Augustin Herrera to rot, be torn to pieces by wild animals or both.

It took an hour to gather enough rocks to bury the body. They placed the family photos they'd found nearby in Augustin's hand. Brett kept the marshal's cell phone. Too bad he didn't have the chance to bury the bodies of his crew. They'd been washed away with the helicopter.

That knot of grief came back, filling his throat until it was difficult to breathe.

"Should we say something?" Eva asked.

"Sure," Brett agreed before taking in a deep breath. "I didn't know Augustin Herrera well—or even at all. I don't know if I should be praying to God or just talking to the universe. But he had a family. He did his job well, and he didn't deserve to die this way. Have mercy on his soul. Have mercy on us all."

"Thank you." She placed her hand on his shoulder. Her touch was soothing and at the same time, left him wanting more. "I'm sure he'd appreciate that you took a few minutes to look after him this way."

He accepted her compliment with a nod. "We really should get going."

The storm clouds had cleared, leaving the sky a deep blue. The downpour had washed away much of the heat, but it wouldn't last for long. Then again, the sun was hanging low on the western horizon. Too soon, they'd be dealing with the dark.

"Which way?" Eva asked.

It was a reasonable question. He just didn't have an answer.

From where they stood, all the hills were more than two miles away. The closest one—and tallest—was to the north. But it was in the opposite direction of the highway and the next town, Encantador. Still, going south meant that they'd have to deal with the creek. Hopefully, once they were out of the valley, his phone would find a signal. "Let's go this way."

They started walking. For the first several minutes neither spoke. Brett assumed that Eva was lost in her own thoughts, much like himself. Now that they were out of the helicopter, it was ludicrous to think that they'd crashed. Wade, Stacy and Lin had been so full of life just hours before. And now they were gone—he didn't even have bodies to mourn over. Even though he knew it wasn't true, it was easier to believe that this was all a bad dream. Any minute, he'd wake up. He'd be back in his house with Eva sleeping next to him.

Maybe this time around, she'd stay for pancakes.

"You know, you can change your outgoing message on your phone. Tell everyone that the helicopter went down and let them know where we've gone."

Brett was startled out of his own head. "What was that?" he asked before processing her words. And then, "You know, that's a great idea."

"Thanks." She smiled. Brett couldn't help himself, and he smiled, too. "The hospital offered a self-defense class last year. The instructor suggested changing our voicemail if we ever had a stranded car. Because even if we don't have any bars, the voicemail is still on."

He stopped walking and pulled his phone from a pocket on his flight suit. It was still in the dry bag. He erased the old message, then spoke into the phone. "This is Brett Wilson, pilot for San Antonio Medical Center." He gave the key information, including the flight number and approximate last known location, then saved the message.

It was followed by a long tone and an automatic voice reply: *Your message was not recorded. Please try again.*

He continued to walk. Eva was at his side. He started over, "This is Brett Wilson…" The second message he recorded was much like the first. He hit the save icon. There was the same tone, the same warning that his message hadn't been saved.

"Dammit," he muttered. The heat of anger began to rise in his chest. "What the hell is wrong with this?"

Eva placed her hand on his arm. Her touch was a balm to soul and soothed away much of his frustration. "It's okay if it doesn't work now. We can try again later."

He looked at the place where her fingertips rested on his flesh. It was like she belonged at his side. Then again, she was a nurse. He imagined she had good bedside manner with all her patients and could calm even the most agitated person.

"Yeah," he said, letting his arm slip away from her touch. "We can try later."

He powered down his phone. There was no need to use up the battery now. Then, he shoved the marshal's phone into the dry bag with his own. It was a tight fit, but he got the closure secure.

He started walking. Eva stayed at his side.

After a moment, he asked, "How's your leg?"

"It's okay. A little painful but not excruciating. Right now, it's not my biggest concern. If we make it back, I'll get someone to look at it."

If we make it back. He reached for her arm, pulling her to a stop. "We'll survive this. There is no 'if we make it back.' It's 'when we get home.'" He squeezed her arm a little tighter. "It'll be okay. I swear."

It was a promise he would keep—no matter what.

Chapter 9

For Eva, climbing to the top of the hill in the desert heat had been difficult. Her legs ached—especially the injury to her calf. Eva worked out a few times a week to keep up her endurance for her shifts, but the wild terrain was nothing like an air-conditioned gym. There was a pull at her side from all the exertion, and she struggled to fill her lungs with air. But if they were able to get a cell signal at the top of the ridge, all the discomfort would be worth it in the end.

She watched as Brett pulled his phone out. He exhaled. "God, I hope this works."

She moved closer. From where she stood, she could see the screen, although it was upside down. He hit the power button, and the device winked to life. He cursed a moment before she saw it.

"No bars," she said, her cheeks and eyes burning.

"No bars," he repeated, then looked at her, his expression softening. "Hey." He rubbed her shoulder. "It's okay. It'll be okay."

He must have been able to read her emotions and knew that she was upset. Then again, Eva had never been blessed with a poker face.

"Okay?" she croaked. Yes, her military training had prepared her for some trying situations. And she'd seen it all as an ER nurse. But they had no idea if Decker was long gone or if he was hiding—and waiting to kill the last two people who could offer an assessment of what had happened after the crash. "How is any of this okay?" She looked over her shoulder, almost expecting to see Decker sneaking up on them from behind. She looked back at Brett. "We have no food. No water. We're twenty miles from the nearest paved road and sixty miles from the next town. And Decker is…somewhere."

Then there was her family who needed her, and she couldn't be there for them.

Brett said nothing, just reached for her hand and pulled Eva into his chest. She leaned into him, not sure if she ever wanted him to let go. After a moment, he said, "Between the two of us, we'll be okay, Eva."

She believed him, and yet she had to ask. "How are you so sure?"

"If we walk toward Encantador, we'll pick up a cell tower eventually. One call will bring the cavalry."

Eva swallowed. "You're right." Although it meant going back the way they'd come. "What about the stream?" She looked at the sky. The sun was close to dipping below the horizon. Even after sunset, it wouldn't be fully dark for hours. But eventually night would arrive. It would get colder—and they didn't have the right gear for hours in the chill. "What about the dark?"

"For now, the sun going down is best. It'll be too hot to walk during midday. And as for the stream…" He exhaled. "We can follow the water until we find a safe place to cross. Besides, if there's no more rain, then the creek will dry up."

She'd lived in this area most of her life and knew his thinking was correct. "I guess we better get going."

"If you need to rest," he said, "we can wait a minute."

"No," she said, shaking her head. "If I sit down now, I might not get back up." Sure, she was joking. But like all humor, there was some truth to what she said. "Let's just keep moving."

They worked their way to the bottom of the hill. Going downhill was easier on her cardiovascular system but harder on her knees and legs. By the time they reached the small valley, her quadriceps and injured shin ached with the same level of pain.

In the distance, she could see the helicopter's tail rotor and part of the hull. From where she stood, it looked like modern art—a statement about man trying to conquer the unceasing desert. She could also see the grave of Augustin Herrera. The sun's last rays cast shadows over the resting place.

"Have I thanked you for saving me?"

"You have," he said. "But there's no need."

"I guess I owe you, don't I?"

"No, you don't." He glanced at her from his periphery. There was something in his look, but she couldn't read his expression. Still, her cheeks warmed under his gaze.

"What is it?" she asked.

He shook his head. "It's nothing."

"Well, obviously, it's something. Go ahead," she urged. "Spit it out."

"Look, you don't owe me any explanations. But we

had such a great connection last night. This morning was another story. I'm just curious what happened."

She glanced away for a moment. If she'd asked him out on a second date after their amazing night together, and he'd sent her that crappy text in response, she'd wonder, too.

She wasn't sure why she'd been so reluctant to tell him how complicated her life was. Her grandmother. Her sister. Moving to Encantador. Maybe because, very early this morning, she hadn't yet been through hell with him and discovered she could count on him.

But that was complicated, too.

Brett hadn't planned on bringing it up at all. But, yeah, he wanted to know. That kind of instant chemistry, with real conversation and mind-blowing sex, was rare. But she clearly had her reasons, and he needed to let it go. "Forget I said anything."

She shook her head. "I should've been honest with you from the beginning. There are things going on in my life—family things." They kept walking. "My grandmother fell yesterday." She exhaled. "It seems like it happened weeks ago, not just a day. Anyway, the fall was bad enough that the doctor said she can't live alone anymore. According to my sister, she refuses to go to an elder care facility. And honestly, if we did try to send her there, she'd be miserable." Eva took in a deep breath and sighed.

He waited a moment to see if she had anything else to say. She didn't. "That's awful," he said. "I'm sorry."

He knew all about families trying to work together to help each other out. "Do you have a plan?"

"The thing is," Eva said, "there's only me and my sister, Katya. She's married with three kids. Right now, her house is bursting at the seams. Adding my grandmother would be too much. I really think there's only one thing I can do."

He already knew what she was going to say. And still, he prodded, "And that is?"

"I'm going to have to relocate to Encantador. There's a hospital in town—the one where we were supposed to land—and they're always short-staffed. I could get a job there."

Her plan was much like the one he expected to hear. It made sense why she didn't want to pursue a relationship. Yet knowing that she wouldn't be in San Antonio anymore hit him like a punch. He shook it off. "I understand completely, Eva. And I admire how devoted you are to your family." That was absolutely true. He was the same way.

That she appreciated what he'd said was clear in her expression. "My grandmother took care of me and Katya after our mother left. She was available when I needed somebody the most. I'm not going to ignore her now." She sighed again. "Anyway, that's why I left this morning, why I texted that there wouldn't be a second date."

"I'm sorry you're stuck here right now. Instead of with your grandmother. I'll do everything in my power to get you to your family."

She reached for his hand and squeezed it. "I believe that. And for the record, I really don't make it a habit to sleep with guys on the first date. It's just not me—usually—but with you…" She scratched the back of her neck as they walked. "Well, you're different. If I was planning on staying in San Antonio, I would've stayed for pancakes."

He smiled. "Your grandmother sounds like an amazing person." He looked at her, as if gauging how personal he could get with a question.

"Ask anything," she said.

"I'm wondering where your mom went."

Eva rarely spoke about her mother. Even though she loved her, their relationship had ended decades before. "I told you that we immigrated to the US from Ukraine. Before that, my father worked at a university in Odessa. He was a professor of world history. My mother had a job in a factory. I'm not even sure what she did, because I was so little, but my memories of my mother are that she was happy. The principal of Encantador High School knew my father. He sponsored my family to come to the US and gave my father a job. My dad spoke English. My sister, Katya, and I grew up in a bilingual home. But my mother never learned the language."

"That must've been lonely for her."

Eva nodded. "As a kid, I didn't see it. She was our mom and was there when my sister and I came home from school. Being enrolled in the public elementary, our English became very good very quickly. 'You're becoming too American,' she would say. Even as a child, I knew it wasn't a compliment. My parents started to argue a lot. They never even bickered in Odessa." She paused, remembering those late nights as her parents screamed at each other from the bedroom. Her father spoke English and her mother Ukrainian.

"What about your dad? What did he think of living in the States?"

"My dad? He loves America—and Texas most of all. It didn't matter that there wasn't a Ukrainian church for miles around. On Sundays, he found a new religion. Football."

Brett barked out a laugh. "Your dad sounds like a good guy."

She paused her story, wondering what her family knew about the crash. Certainly, they'd all heard by now, and what was more, they'd be worried. How had her grandmother taken the news? Eva didn't want the crash to be what caused her baba's health to fail.

"My dad is great," she continued after a pause that was too long. She quickly added, "My mom is great, too. It's just that America wasn't the place for her. After five years of being miserable, my dad sent her back to Odessa for a visit. Katya and I both wanted to go with her. After all, there was family we wanted to see, too. She refused to take us. Refused to even consider it. Before she left, I think I knew that she wasn't coming back." That familiar knot of grief filled her throat. Her eyes stung, and she blinked hard. It had been years since she'd cried over her mother, but here she was with her eyes watering.

"Anyway," she croaked. "She moved back to Odessa and filed for a divorce. After a few years, she remarried. My mom and her second husband have three other children."

"That must have been really hard on you," Brett said, sympathy in his voice.

It was. Her mother going back to Ukraine was the reason she never felt as if she had a home.

"It's not easy for me to talk about all this, but I'm glad I did. I'm pretty talked out, though," she added. She liked the idea of walking in silence for a bit, having his quiet, strong presence beside her.

He squeezed her hand in acknowledgment and didn't say another word. Another of those gestures that made her feel…special to him.

Walking silently turned out to be a good thing. Brett had to focus on what was important, and that was getting them home. They'd returned to where they started at the creek, next to the crash site. Water, dark and muddy, still swirled in the riverbed. A slice of the dry bank fell into the water and was washed away.

He scanned the horizon, looking for a safe place to cross. There was none. "Let's stick to the bank. We're heading in the general direction we want to go. Eventually, we can get to the other side."

Eva faced west and held her hand up. Her palm was flat and facing her. "We have three hours until sunset," she said. He knew the old trick of measuring the time by the distance of the sun to the horizon. "That means it's five o'clock, give or take a few minutes. They have to know we're missing. The helicopter was due to land at three thirty."

She was right. By now, a search party had been dispatched to find them. But they'd go to the helicopter's homing beacon. That meant they'd be looking in the wrong place. He didn't need to add that extra bit—especially since they both knew it was true. "I'm sure people are trying to find us right now."

"Maybe if we stick to the riverbed, we'll find the helicopter," she said. "Then, they'll find us, too."

Walking slowly, he watched the water eddy hypnotically. Eva was a pace in front of him. Her limp, which hadn't been bad before, was more pronounced. "Your leg looks like it hurts. Do you need to rest?"

"Like I said before, if I sit down now, I won't get back up."

"It's also true that if you reinjure yourself or make your injury worse, then we might not be going anywhere."

"Hey." She placed her hands on her hips in mock indignation. "I'm the nurse. I'm the one who gets to give the serious talks about health."

He allowed himself a chuckle.

She continued, "But you're right. I could use a break."

He pointed to a stone that sat on the ground ten yards ahead. "You can rest over there."

She hobbled to the sandstone boulder. Easing down on the flat top, she moaned. God help him, it was the same noise she made while they were having sex.

"That's the best," she said.

Setting the med kit next to her feet, Brett shook the feeling back into his hand. "You rest for a few more minutes, I'm going to scout the bank and see if there's any place for us to cross."

He walked along the bank, watching the dark and

swirling water as it rushed past. The movement of the water was almost peaceful and gave him a moment of clarity. He appreciated the fact that she'd been honest about her situation. And her commitment to her family really did move him.

He'd promised her he'd get her to them. And he would.

Chapter 10

Brett scanned the river, up and downstream, looking for a way to cross. So far, the only thing he'd seen was water, silty and full of debris. The branches of a low-hanging bush hung in the torrent. He glanced at the twigs and leaves caught in the muddy foam. Then, he looked back. His eyes had seen something that his mind had missed.

There, in the middle of the debris, was the carton of ready-made meals from the helicopter. The cardboard box was double wrapped in plastic and bobbed as the current pushed it into the branches.

"Come here," he shouted, waving to Eva. "I've found something."

Panting, she walked toward him. She held the med kit by the handle, and it slapped her thigh with each lurching step.

"How's your leg?" he asked.

"Doesn't hurt. The boot's awkward, but I'm glad I have it."

He was relieved she wasn't in pain.

She was looking out at the water. "What is that?"

"The rations," he said. Sure, it wasn't much. Just four sets of breakfast, lunch and dinner. But if everything in the box had stayed dry, it'd be safe to eat. At the thought of food, his stomach contracted painfully. "I need a stick or something to pull the box close enough to reach."

"If a stick helps us get something to eat, I'll find a whole damn tree," she said. "You know, I was supposed to have pancakes for breakfast."

He looked at her.

She gave him a wink to show that she was teasing.

He shook his head.

"Too soon?" she asked, setting the medical kit on the ground.

He liked the easy rapport that they'd developed. It was one of the reasons he'd wanted to make love to her after the first date. It was also why it still stung that the relationship was over before it began. "Yeah." He chuckled to show he was teasing, as well. "Too soon."

Eva walked along the bank, heading back the way they'd just come. Brett took a few steps in the opposite direction. He hadn't even started to look when she called out, "I think this will work."

She held up a twisted branch, almost a yard long. Even better, one end split into a fork. He met her as she walked back toward him. "That's perfect," he said, reaching for the stick.

His fingers grazed the back of her hand. He needed to ignore the electricity that shot from his fingertips and up his arm, but it was damn difficult.

Standing on the edge of the riverbank, he reached out with the stick. He touched the top of the box, pulling it free of the branches. "When it gets close, you'll have to get it out of the water."

She knelt next to where he stood. "I'm ready."

He pulled on the stick, moving the box closer and closer. The current pulled against the carton, trying to drag it downstream. Brett kept the pressure on the top of the box, careful to pull it to him without breaking the seal and ruining everything inside. "Just a few inches more," he said, speaking more to himself than Eva. "Get ready."

And then, the box dipped, sinking under the surface. It bobbed back up, inexplicably several feet away. Sweat dampened his brow and pooled at the nape of his neck. He couldn't lose the rations. Having food was the difference between life and death. He reached out farther. Then a little more.

He felt the bank crumble a moment before the earth splashed into the water. Brett went with it.

In an instant, he was in water up to his chest. The current buffeted him from all sides. The water swirled around his legs, trying to upend him and pull him into the murky depths.

On the bank, Eva stretched out her hand. "Grab a hold of me. I'll pull you to the shore."

Getting out of the water was the prudent thing to do, he knew that. But he wasn't about to let the rations get away. He reached out with the stick, catching the box on the top. He pulled it to him, then grabbed it in his hands. He shoved the box toward Eva. "Take this."

"Give me your hand," she insisted.

He ignored her demand and pushed the box closer. "Take it. I can't climb out and carry the box at the same time."

Eva muttered a curse, but she dragged the box through

the water and lifted it onto the shore. "Now you," she said, leaning back over the creek. "Give me your hand."

Brett took a step forward. And another. Eva was so close that he could almost reach her hand—almost, but not quite. He moved his foot forward once more and plummeted into the murky depths.

The water was freezing cold and black as midnight. The current swept him off his feet, pushing him downstream and keeping him submerged. He tried to gauge where he was, but he couldn't even tell what was riverbed and what was sky.

His mouth filled with water, cutting off breath, and Eva's face flashed through his mind.

If he drowned in this stupid river, Eva would be alone. The only way they could survive in the desert was if they stayed together.

He had to focus. He had to live.

Long ago, he'd been trained on what to do in this exact situation. The steps he needed to take came back to him at last. Brett stopped moving and let his feet follow the current. Then he held on to his knees. Slowly, he started to rise. He could see light breaking through the darkness. He kicked his legs and reached out with his arms. After breaking through the surface, he sucked in a lungful of air.

The first thing he saw was Eva. She was kneeling on the bank and scanning the water. Her face was pinched with concern. "Omigod," she said. "I thought you were gone for good."

Of all the things that surprised Brett, the one that struck him most was how little he'd traveled underwater.

He was only a few yards from where he'd gone under. "I'm harder to get rid of than all that," he said with more bravado than he felt.

Eva leaned forward, holding the end of the stick. "Can you reach this?"

Brett stretched out, careful to maintain his footing. His fingertips brushed the end of the branch. He pulled himself forward. Then he grabbed hold with his whole hand.

From the bank, Eva dragged him toward her and dry land.

In seconds, he was close enough to touch her. Reaching out, he placed his palm into hers, her grip strong but soft. She pulled, and finally Brett made it to the edge of the river. He lifted himself out of the water.

Kneeling on the bank, he was suddenly exhausted. He rolled to his back and listened to his heartbeat.

"Jeez, I thought I'd lost you." She brushed the hair from his forehead. He relaxed under her touch. "It was terrifying to think that you were gone—that I'd never see you again." She exhaled, an unmistakable tremble in her breath. "I should give you an antibiotic, just as a precaution. Who knows what's in that water."

He lay on his back and stared at the sky as Eva retrieved the medical kit and returned to him. She held a pill in her hand. "Take this."

He lifted onto his elbow and, placing the medication on his tongue, forced the pill down his throat.

"How are you?" she asked.

"That depends," he said. "If the food is intact, then it was all worth it."

"Let's see." Using a utility knife that hung from her

flight suit, Eva sliced through the plastic wrapping, wadded it up and shoved it into her pocket. "The box looks dry."

"Let's see what's inside," he said.

She sliced through the seam of tape, opening the box. "Looks like granola bars. Cereal. Apple sauce in a cup. There's other stuff, too." She held up a granola bar. "You want one?"

He took it and tore through the wrapper, his stomach gurgling.

That was when he heard it—a rumble rolling across the plain and echoing off the surrounding hills.

Eva turned her face skyward. "Great," she mumbled. "If there's thunder, more rain is coming."

But Brett had served full-time in the army. He'd been deployed to combat zones more than once. The noise wasn't thunder. His blood was like ice in his veins. "That's not another storm," he said. "That's gunfire."

Eva stared at him, her eyes wide with fear or disbelief, he couldn't tell which.

Before either could say a word, there was another report. The ground exploded in a cloud of dirt and stone as the bullet struck near their feet.

Decker looked down the sites of his gun as sweat dripped from his hairline and burned his eyes. His vision was blurry. His whole body ached, as if thousands of angry wasps had been let loose under his skin. It was no wonder that he couldn't shoot for crap. He wanted— make that *needed*—his meds.

He'd watched the nurse—he remembered her name was Eva—and the guy who was probably the pilot for over an hour now. When he'd seen their figures moving across the plain, he'd planned to avoid them altogether. But then he noticed the red cross emblazoned on the box that the guy carried. He knew it was a medical kit of some kind and that meant painkillers were inside.

He had to get that med kit. But how? With his damned headache—like his skull was being squeezed in a vise— he couldn't think.

Already two bullets had been wasted. He couldn't afford to fire and miss again.

The prudent thing to do was let them run. Chasing after the duo wasted time he didn't have. But that med kit was better than a treasure chest. Besides, he wouldn't make it all the way to Mexico if he couldn't concentrate because of his pain—not to mention the withdrawal symptoms from not getting his regular dose of meds. All he needed was a little something to take the edge off.

In missing his shots, he'd lost the element of surprise. Those two knew he was armed and looking for them. He drew in a deep breath and tried to think like people on the run. Their only chance of survival would be to get to the highway, which was roughly twenty miles to the south.

That meant he knew where they were going. He need not waste any more bullets trying to kill them from afar. All he needed to do was watch and wait. His headache eased a bit.

Decker was once again the predator, and he was ready to stalk his prey.

Using their contacts with the Texas Rangers, the team from Texas Law found a helicopter that was willing to pick them up in Encantador and take them to the last known location of the missing medevac helicopter. The chopper had room for four people. The pilot and one passenger in the front, along with two seats in the back.

Ryan sat next to the pilot, a woman named Farrah Kaufman. She spoke into a mic attached to her helmet and broadcast through the headsets that he and Isaac wore. "We've got a location for the downed chopper's black box. Just a few minutes more. There's a field nearby, and we can land."

Just like the pilot predicted, the remainder of the flight only took minutes. They circled above a small clearing, and even from the air, Ryan could see the remains of the helicopter. It lay on its side in the bottom of a ravine, covered in dirt, turning the once white aircraft to gray. A trickle of water flowed around either side of the hull as if the chopper was a great metal island.

"Christ Almighty," Isaac whispered into his mic. "What the hell happened?"

That was what Ryan wanted to know. The back rotor was missing along with the rear section of the hull.

"Don't know," said Farrah. "Maybe the helicopter got pushed here by the river. There was a big storm that blew through here not too long ago. When that happens, every crevasse can become a raging river."

Ryan nodded. "How'd it even get in the water? And where is everyone?"

"That's what we're going to find out," said Isaac.

The pilot brought the aircraft to the ground. The minute that the skids touched the dirt, Ryan and Isaac unfastened their harnesses and opened the cargo door. The downdraft from the rotor washed over them, the roar of the engine deafening.

Ducking low, Ryan jumped to the ground and ran to the wrecked aircraft, his stomach twisting into a knot. Isaac was at his heels.

Approaching the helicopter, his sprint slowed, then he stopped altogether. From the looks of it, Farrah had been right, and the helicopter had been submerged. Mud was caked in the hold. The windscreen was broken. He peered into the torn rear fuselage. There was a body, male and tall, tangled in cargo netting. Ryan's heart slammed into his ribs, and he jumped back.

"What is it?"

He swallowed, trying to slow his racing pulse. "Looks like there are fatalities."

Isaac approached, then exhaled and shook his head.

"Can you tell," Ryan began, "if they died during the crash or was it a deliberate act?"

He knew that Isaac wasn't a medical examiner, but the investigator had seen his share of gruesome deaths.

"We'll have to leave that to the coroner," Isaac said. "I'm going to ask Farrah to radio in that we need an ME," said Isaac. "Hold up, and I'll be right back."

"Sure thing," Ryan said, even though he had no intention of waiting. He had to know about Decker. Was he the cause of the crash or another victim?

As soon as Isaac sprinted away, Ryan moved forward. He entered the helicopter through the jagged hole at the back. The floor of the hold was filled with water, a sheen of fuel shimmering on the surface. He saw a second body, face down in a puddle. Even without seeing a face, Ryan could tell from the flight suit and build that it wasn't Decker.

He moved away from the body, toward the cockpit. There was a female, also dead. Bile rose in the back of his throat. He coughed and looked away.

"What the hell are you doing in there?" Isaac yelled from the rear of the helicopter. "You can't contaminate the scene."

Ryan carefully walked to the back of the hold. "I had to know, man," he said, stepping into the sun. "I needed to find out if Decker was in the helicopter or not."

"And?" Isaac asked.

A sick feeling settled in Ryan's stomach as he shook his head. "There are three dead bodies in there." He'd seen the flight manifest. On board were two pilots, male and female, a female nurse, two male EMTs, the patient they were transporting—Decker Newcombe—and the US marshal sent to guard the patient. Even though it was obvious, he said, "That means four people are missing."

Isaac cursed before flicking his fingers toward the wreckage. "What are the chances that anyone made it out of that crash alive?"

"If we're talking about Decker," Ryan said, "then the odds are pretty damn good."

"The guy's like a cat with nine lives. How many has he used up already? Seven? Or is it eight?"

Ryan used to be friends with Decker—or as close as anyone could come to being friends with a sociopath. He couldn't count how many times the other man should've perished, but he never did. Then again, Ryan was the most recent person to spare the killer's miserable life.

Decker had tried to commit a murder online, a crime that Ryan had interrupted. In the ensuing chaos, Decker had been shot and was stuck in a burning warehouse.

Ryan could've left him behind.

But he hadn't.

He pulled the murderer from the flames and got him medical care. Now, his former friend was on the loose and as dangerous and deadly as ever.

If he was going to stop him, he had to focus.

Which brought up another point. Issac was right. The crash had totaled the helicopter, and the wreckage had been caught in a flash flood—that was the only thing that could've pushed the aircraft downstream. Even an evil bastard like Decker didn't stand much of a chance.

"C'mon," Isaac said. "Let's follow the streambed. That way we can see if there are any other bodies lost in the water."

Ryan nodded as if in agreement.

Isaac was a good person. A much better person than Ryan would ever be, even on his best day. Because of that, Ryan didn't bother to inform his boss that his top priority wasn't to find any other victims of the crash.

He only wanted to locate Decker's cold corpse. And this time, he'd make sure that he stayed dead.

Chapter 11

Eva ran, cursing with each step. It was the damned medical boot. Sure, the air cast stabilized her injured leg, but it made her slower than usual and clumsy. The hard plastic rubbed against her flesh and with each step, she could feel blisters forming. The med kit slapped against her thigh and hip, but at least she had it. The worst was the injury itself. Pain stabbed into her ankle and radiated upward until her teeth hurt.

But she ignored all the discomfort and ran. It didn't matter how much her foot bothered her; it was nothing compared to what would happen if she was struck by a bullet.

Holding the box of food in one arm and her free hand in the other, Brett pulled her along. The stream was on her left and the open plain on her right. Ahead was a thick willow tree. It didn't provide much protection, but at least it gave them some cover.

Decker was out there, somewhere.

"Get down," said Brett as they skidded behind the branches.

Eva gulped air, the same way she used to drink from a garden hose when she was a kid.

"How are you?" asked Brett. His hair was damp from the creek. Otherwise, he wasn't even breathing hard.

"I'm fine," she panted.

"Are you sure? You didn't get shot, obviously. How's your leg?"

"Fine," she said again, the single word a wheeze. "You know..." she sucked in a breath "...if I survive this, I'm going to get in shape."

"What do you mean? You look pretty good to me."

Despite the circumstances, his compliment started a new round of fluttering in her stomach. But she pushed aside all thoughts of past and future. What she needed was a plan for right now. "What're we going to do?"

Brett sat back on his haunches and exhaled. She'd noticed that about him. Whenever he was thinking, he let out a long breath. Almost like he was letting go of any bad ideas. "We can't sit here all night and wait for Decker to come find us."

"Agreed."

"We also have to go south, toward Encantador, or at least find the highway."

She nodded her head, saving her breath.

He paused for a moment. "We can cross here," he said. "The creek's already drying up. I hate to come out where Decker can see us. But walking on this side of the streambed makes us an easier target." He inclined his head to the opposite bank. "At least over there, we have cover, and we're getting closer to town."

A big part of Eva wanted to stay behind the willow tree. But Brett was right. Staying where they were made them an easy target. If she was going to have to face the likes of Decker Newcombe, it wouldn't be because she was cowering behind a bush. "Okay," she said, sitting up taller. "When do we go?"

"We'll wait a bit. We can both use the rest." Brett held out his granola bar. The wrapper was crumpled from where he'd clutched it in his palm. "Take some. We both need energy, and who knows when we'll be able to eat again."

She held out her hand, and he poured the broken pieces into her palm. For a moment, they both ate in silence. Too soon, she chewed the last piece of granola; her mouth was dry. Not for the first time, she wished that they had found the case of water, as well.

The longer they sat behind the tree, the less she wanted to cross the creek and climb another hill. It was the only way to get home, but they'd be exposed. Before losing her nerve, she said, "We should go now."

Brett peered through the low-hanging branches, scanning the hillside. He stood, holding the box of food in one arm. He gripped the med kit's handle with the other hand. Finally, he said, "Let's go."

Her heartbeat raced, thrumming at the base of her skull. She followed Brett, stepping from behind the relative safety of the tree. He was tall, his shoulders broad. If Decker shot at them again, it would be Brett who would take the bullet.

The thought that he might die left her eyes burning. It was more than being alone and lost—although that would be bad enough. It was that the world would be a worse place without him in it.

"I'll go first," he said, standing on the bank. "If anything happens…"

"Don't," she interrupted. She couldn't have him speak disaster into being. As if to counter his thought, she said, "Nothing bad will happen."

He turned to look at her. "Then be careful."

"Brett." She reached for his arm and placed her lips on his cheek. The kiss was over as soon as it began, and yet her pulse raced. "For luck," she said.

He held her gaze for a moment, but she couldn't read his expression. "Thanks." He turned.

"Brett," she called out again. There was so much she wanted to say to him—that she was happy they'd met. She had enjoyed their one night together. And sincerely, she was sorry that it wouldn't work out between them. When he turned to face her again, she couldn't find the right words. Instead, she held out her palm. "I'll carry the med kit."

"You sure?"

"Just hand it over."

He gave it to her, then gently squeezed her wrist. "It'll all work out."

She tried to smile and gripped the handle tighter. "I hope you're right."

Turning, he stepped into the water and started to wade into the current. The stream came up to his ankles. His calves. His thighs. When he was submerged to his waist, he lifted the box of food overhead. Eva followed, clutching the med kit to her chest. The water swirled around her legs, pushing her downstream with each step. It was colder than she expected, and within seconds, her feet were numb.

Brett reached the opposite bank and climbed out of the water. If he could do it, she could, as well. Back in college, when she'd been with the Air Guard, she'd been trained what to do in case of a water landing. But that was years ago, and the lessons were fuzzy. Still, she tried to remember what she'd been taught. Filling her lungs with a deep breath, she focused on each step. The water crept up her legs. It leaked into the boot she wore on her injured foot. She tried not think about what might be floating in the water, or who might be watching them.

Then the current was up to her waist. It filled her flight suit. For an instant, she felt pain as an imaginary bullet tore a hole through her shoulder. She knew that trying to make their way to civilization was the only way to survive. But being this vulnerable left her hands trembling.

When the water reached her chest, she balanced the med kit on her head. The current was strong. One wrong step, and she'd get dragged underwater. Still, she wasn't going to turn back. Which meant there was no way to go other than forward. She took another step.

Just as the creek bed dipped down in the middle, it rose on the opposite side. The water receded. Chest, stomach, thighs and calves.

She splashed out of the water, clawing clods of dirt as she scrambled up the embankment. Dropping the med kit, she bent over and held on to her knees. Only then did she remember to draw a breath.

"Hey." Brett placed his strong hand on her shoulder. "What's the matter?"

"Decker is getting to me. It's been a while since I was a part of a military unit. Sometimes I can still call up my training, and my fear abates. But a serial killer shooting at me while I'm exposed crossing a stream?" She stood up straight. The water that had filled her flight suit poured onto the ground until she was standing in a puddle. The fabric clung to her like a second skin. "I just got scared there for a minute."

"Understandable," he said, glancing at her with concern. "If you're okay, we should get going. It's twenty miles to the highway, and that's a lot of walking. I want to get up and over this ridgeline before it gets dark."

She nodded and looked around. No serial killers in sight, but for all they knew, Decker was watching and waiting for the right moment to strike again.

With Eva at his side, Brett had been walking for hours. Luckily, his smartwatch still worked, and he could tell that they'd hiked over four miles.

The sun had dipped below the horizon, leaving the sky a riot of colors. Pink. Orange. And at the edges, purple. The ground, however, had been leached of color and definition. Missteps could happen easily. Eva had already injured her ankle; they couldn't afford another wound.

"Can I ask you a question?" she said as they descended a hill.

He wasn't in the mood to converse, but the sound of her voice soothed him in a way nothing else had before. "You can ask me anything."

"Have you ever been part of a search-and-rescue team?"

He nodded. "I have."

"Can you tell me what's probably going on with the team out looking for us?"

"Well," he began, "I imagine that they've located the chopper's black box by now. If they've found the bodies of the crew, they might think we're dead, as well. They'll figure that we were pushed out of the aircraft by the floodwaters."

"So, nobody's looking for us now?"

"They'll conduct an aerial search, certainly. At least for a few days."

"And then what?" she asked, her voice small.

"Before then, we'll get found. Or we'll pick up cell service and make a call."

"I feel like you're lying to me," she said.

He was. Brett had no clue if or when they'd find cell coverage in the middle of nowhere. A plane would definitely be searching for them, but spotting him and Eva while they were trying to hide from a serial killer would be difficult. The two of them couldn't exactly walk out in the open, waving up at the skies at the first sight of an aircraft. Not unless they wanted Decker to know where they were hidden—which they did not.

He didn't respond. In the world of uncertainties, there was one thing he knew. He'd do anything to protect Eva, even if it was from the awful truth.

"You know that I can handle this situation, right? You know that if you aren't upfront with me, I can't be any help. In fact, I'll only be a burden." She paused. "I grew up around here. I know that cell coverage is spotty at best. I know that there's a lot of ground to cover to look for someone who's gone missing. Plus, you didn't mention the serial killer with a gun."

He exhaled, putting one foot in front of the other as they climbed another steep incline. "I think our only chance of survival is finding the interstate—and then, a friendly motorist who'll give us a ride."

She frowned. "So, you're saying that our chances are basically crap."

He wasn't about to give up or give in. "So long as we're alive, there's always a chance."

"I admire your optimism, Brett," she said, her voice reedy. "But I don't know that I buy it. Me, I'm more of a realist, with a toe across the line into pessimism. It happens when you work in the emergency department."

"In a situation like this, we always need to hold on to hope."

"Sounds like something from the inside of a greeting card," she said. "Maybe you should look into a second career."

"See, you're being optimistic, too. If you didn't think we're going to make it, then there wouldn't be any reason for a second career."

She barked out a laugh and then grimaced. Holding her side, she said, "Don't make jokes. It's hard enough to climb all these damn hills without laughing."

They crested the top of the rise. Night was closing in from all sides. The last remnant of the sun was only a sliver of orange on the western horizon. Brett stopped and inhaled. The air was loamy and heavy with humidity. Wiping the sweat from his brow, he scanned the sky. There were no early stars, only clouds. "I think we're going to get another storm before morning."

Eva cursed. "The only good thing with that is we can try to collect some rainwater."

"Now you're definitely being an optimist. I knew I'd rub off on you."

She chuckled. "Let's see what's in the case of food. Maybe there's something we can eat now and use the container to catch water."

"There is," he said, confident that he remembered what was inside the box. He set the case on the ground and squatted next to it. His quadriceps burned but the stretch would be good for his thighs. After all, they had miles yet to travel. He removed a plastic cup filled with applesauce. He held it up to Eva. "Here you go."

She peeled back the foil lid and tipped her head, dumping the contents into her mouth. He found a second applesauce pouch and quickly depleted it.

She held out the empty cup to Brett. "We better keep moving. Once it starts to rain, we won't be able to go anywhere."

He knew she was right. He placed both cups back in the box and lifted it. She picked up the med kit next to her feet. "Let's go," he said.

As they began to walk, he knew that their chances of being found were slim. But it wasn't because people weren't looking. Part of him wanted to leave a trail for the search team to follow, even just the two empty applesauce pouches. But Decker might spot the litter first.

And kill them long before they'd ever be found.

* * *

The storm came sooner and with more violence than Eva imagined. She and Brett had just descended a hill and were walking through a narrow pass when the first fat drop hit her cheek. As she wiped the drip away, the water still clinging to her hand, the deluge began.

She held the med kit over her head. "Where the hell did that come from?" she asked. Then, "Forget I asked. I've learned all I want to know about sudden storms."

Brett nodded his grim agreement. They were both silent for a moment, and she had no doubt he was also thinking of the crew he'd lost and the marshal. Finally, he said, "We gotta get to higher ground."

He was right. If this storm dropped as much water as the one that downed the helicopter, then they risked getting caught by another flash flood.

Tucking the box of food under one arm, he held out his hand to her. "Come with me."

She swiped the rainwater from her face, then reached for him.

He held her palm tightly against his own and, leading her over ground now slick with mud, began to climb the next hill. It was steep, the ground uneven. Climbing up this hill would be difficult in the best of circumstances— and in the dark and in the middle of a storm, these conditions were far from the best.

Her toe caught on the edge of a stone. She pitched forward, landing hard on her hands and knees. The med kit hit the ground and tumbled backwards, end over end before coming to rest on its side.

"Dammit," she cursed, rising to her feet.

"You okay?"

Her knees ached. By morning, she'd be stiff and covered with bruises. Her injured leg burned, the ibuprofen she'd taken earlier had worn off. Her hands were raw and bloody. "I'm fine," she lied. It would do no good to complain about minor injuries. "Let me get the kit."

She turned, careful about her footing, and climbed down the hill to where the med kit lay. With a groan, she picked it up. When she stood, she stared into the darkness. Had there been something there in the shadows? A man? Gooseflesh rose on her arms as she strained to see into the storm. There was nothing. Now.

But had Decker been there and darted into the shadows? She quickly turned around, needing to see where Brett was.

Brett was closing the distance between them. "I think there's a cave right behind you."

She looked into the gloom again. There, ten yards away, was what she had seen. She wiped at her eyes again. Now that she knew what she was looking for, it was easy to pick out. The rock formation was about six feet tall, but—she laughed quietly—how had she mistaken that for a person?

Brett stood above her on the hill and pointed to the cave. "C'mon. We can at least get out of this weather."

Eva scrambled up behind him. For moment, she thought about all the critters—none of them friendly—who might also take shelter in the cave. She pushed the thought away.

Brett must've been thinking the same thing. When she reached the mouth of the cavern, he'd already pulled out his phone and was using the flashlight to scan the space. It wasn't much, just a few feet of sandy ground. But it was thankfully empty and dry. He glanced at the screen. "Still no bars," he said before powering down the device. "Let's get inside."

She ducked down to keep from hitting her head on an overhanging rock. Once inside the cave, she could stand up, but there wasn't much more room than that. If she pressed one shoulder against a wall, she'd be able to touch the other side with an outstretched arm.

She set down the med kit and shook feeling back into her hand. Brett set down the box of food. The cardboard was starting to pucker from the rain.

"There were a few little plastic cups in there," he said, rummaging in the box. "We can use them to collect rainwater."

She knelt on the ground to help. The cups were stacked in a corner. She pulled out two and handed them to Brett. "Here you go."

Standing in the cave, he held both cups out into the downpour. It took only moments for them to fill with rainwater. He handed her a full cup, and she threw it back like a shot of alcohol.

It hit her stomach like a bomb, and for a minute, her middle contracted painfully. "I should've known better," she said, gripping her side, "and drank slowly."

"Here." He held out his own cup. "Sip this."

"I can't take your water."

He held his hand out to the sky. "I think there's plenty more where that came from."

She laughed. "You're right." She passed him the empty cup while taking the one that was full.

Brett kept his body in the cave, arm once again outstretched into the rain. While the other cup filled, she sipped the water. It was cool and refreshing. Soon, Brett lifted a full cup in salute. "Cheers."

She waited as he sipped the water. Once he was finished, she said, "Give me the cup. I'll refill them both."

"I got this," he said.

She held out her hand. "My arms can be in the rain. It's only fair. And it's not like my boot can get any wetter."

He opened his mouth, ready to argue. Obviously, he was raised to be a courteous man. But she was a force on her own. She'd taken care of herself her whole life. Sure, it was tempting to rest while he got wet. But she wasn't about to give into any weaknesses now.

He handed her his cup. "If you insist."

"I do."

Unfortunately, her arms weren't long enough for her to stand under the rock ledge and still have her hands in the rain. It meant that more of her had to get wet. The water had long ago washed away the sweat, the grime and the heat of the day. Now, it was just cold and unpleasant.

With both cups filled, she handed one to Brett. "Drink up."

"I think you said something like that last night when they brought a margarita to the table."

"Did I?" she asked, sipping the water. As long as the rain held, they'd be able to stay hydrated. Tomorrow would be another day, but for now, they were okay. "God, last night feels like it happened to a different person."

Settling on the ground, she unstrapped the Velcro that kept her air cast in place. She took it off, hoping the boot might dry quickly. With a sigh, she wiggled her toes.

"How's the leg?"

"I don't think anything's broken." Without the boot, her shin throbbed with each beat of her heart. Her skin tightened as the injury began to swell. "Still hurts like hell."

"How about some more ibuprofen?"

"Definitely." She unlocked the med kit's latch, finding the OTC pain meds in a foil packet. She washed them down with the last swallow of rainwater. There were also bandages for the blisters and antiseptic wipes to prevent infection.

"I'll fill that up again." Brett took the cup from her hand. His fingers grazed hers.

Despite the pain, the fear and the exhaustion, her heart skipped a beat.

"Thanks," she said, not daring to meet his eye. Because if she did, would he see how much she still wanted him?

Chapter 12

For the next thirty minutes, the rain continued to fall. Brett switched back and forth with Eva, sharing the job of collecting rainwater one cup at a time. Even as the downpour continued, he went from parched to sated to overfull.

"When I went to basic training," he said as the downpour eased into a drizzle, "we were told that hydration was the most important part of staying alive."

Shaking her head, she gave a quiet laugh. "I remember basic training. It was brutal."

"You didn't like it?" Brett asked. "I kinda thought it was fun. Like scouting on steroids."

She smiled. "Times ten for me. But I actually loved getting pushed to my limits, learning what I was capable of—more than I ever would have thought at eighteen. I might have pursued an air force career, but I was always so worried about my family. Baba needed me, Katya had a lot on her shoulders... It was hard to leave after my service, but I did get to serve, and I know I made the right choice for my family."

Funny, Brett hadn't thought about college for years. After graduating high school in Dallas, he'd gone to school at Texas Midland State College. His first year, he'd had too much fun, and his grades suffered. His father, an attorney and a stern man at best, refused to pay for school if his son was going to, quote, "screw around." He'd given Brett a choice, go into the military or get a job.

Brett enlisted the summer of his twentieth birthday. In the army, he found more than just the discipline his father wanted; he found his life's passion—flight.

Of course, he also learned some important lessons during basic training. One was to eat whenever he had a chance.

"Are you hungry?" he asked. "How about a little box of dry Cheerios?"

Eva pressed a hand to her stomach. "Actually, I'm not sure how hungry I am. Though under the circumstances I guess I should eat something. Especially since I took some meds."

He rummaged through their food supply, pulled out the small box of Cheerios, then looked at her. "Tell you what—how about we share it, since you're not hungry? Then if you decide you want something else, we'll dive into another bag."

She shrugged. "Sure."

He opened the box and shook some into her hand. They ate, split one more pouch of applesauce, and he felt more or less satisfied for now.

Eva looked better, too, with more of a sparkle back in her eyes now that she was full, hydrated and not getting rained on.

"Well," he said. "We're here for the night. We'll keep walking in the morning."

"Sounds good." Eva sat with her back to one wall of the cave. She'd bandaged her own blisters and was keeping her injured ankle out of the air cast for now. "I didn't realize how tired I was until I sat down."

"You get some sleep," he said. "I'll take first watch."

She opened her mouth, ready to argue. Before she said a word, he held up his palms. "I'll wake you in a few hours," he promised. "Then I'll catch some sleep."

She gave him a weary smile. "Thanks."

Standing at the mouth of the cave, he took a minute to assess their surroundings. Calling it a cave was a bit of an overstatement. It was more of a narrow gap in the middle of a rock formation. But it provided them with some cover from the elements.

He stepped outside. The air was cool and clear. Folding his arms across his chest, Brett inhaled deeply and looked—as he always did—toward the sky.

The clouds had moved away, leaving an ebony carpet filled with diamonds. He found the Big Dipper. The Little Dipper and the North Star. Staring into the darkness, he fixed north in his mind. To get to the interstate, they had to go south by southeast. He took another step into the night and turned in that direction.

He stared into the darkness—watching and listening. There were no sounds. No sights.

Wait. That wasn't right. On the horizon, in the direction of the highway, he saw a golden glow. The light was faint, but there, nonetheless.

He stared at it for a moment and then, a moment more.

It was moving through his field of vision from left to right. His heart began to slam into his chest.

Were those headlights on a moving vehicle?

They had to be. If he were forced to guess, it was most likely something large like a long-haul trucker. But it meant that they were headed in the right direction.

Brett did a little quick math. On flat ground, the horizon was approximately three miles away. It was night, pitch dark, and he had the benefit of elevation, which meant the road was farther.

He estimated that it was at least a dozen miles to the interstate. None of it was flat ground and there were more hills to climb. But the thing was, it could be done.

He wanted to let out a victorious whoop.

But it made no sense to call out, letting Decker know where they were. He turned around, retracing his steps to the cave.

Eva looked up as he entered. "What is it?" she asked, her voice a whisper.

He knelt next to her. "I saw it," he said, whispering the words into her ear. "I found the highway from the ridgeline. It's not going to be easy, but it's doable. How's your ankle?"

"It hurt," she said, "but I can walk."

The idea of leaving now was tempting. But with Decker out there, somewhere, he knew it was best to stay hidden. It gave them time for the killer to lose their trail completely. "We'll leave with first light."

Sitting up, she drew her thighs into her chest, resting her chin on her knees. He sat next to her, his shoulder pressed against hers.

His pulse continued to race, but this time, it had nothing to do with being close to a murderer. Now, it was all about Eva.

After a while, he traced the back of her hand and leaned in close. "You can go back to sleep," he said, his voice low.

"Sleep?" she echoed in a whisper. "I won't be able to get any more rest. Not right now, at least."

"I'm sorry I woke you." He whispered the word into her hair. "I was just excited about the road, you know?"

She nodded her head. He could feel the movement on his chest. Feel her breath on his skin. He wrapped an arm around her shoulder, and she leaned into his chest. Without any thought, Brett placed his lips on the top of her head.

She tilted up her face just slightly, her gaze meeting his. God, she was beautiful. Bending to her, he placed his lips on hers. She sighed and he deepened the kiss.

Brett's kiss sent a bolt of lightning straight to Eva's middle. Tonight, here in this cave, they were safe. There'd been no sign of the killer. No sound. She had barely relaxed, but as time passed, she wasn't as tense.

All she wanted was to let loose again, be distracted from everything. And she well knew that Brett Wilson could make that happen.

They'd talked about where they stood. If Brett had kissed her, it meant they were on the same page. That he needed this, too.

Without another thought, she broke away from the kiss. Rising to her knees, she placed her hand over her zipper to muffle any noise out of an abundance of caution. Then, she opened the front of her flight suit. She shrugged out of the sleeves and pulled the fabric down to her waist.

Using her thumb, she traced his mouth. She wanted to tell him that having him in her life, even if it was just for a few days, had been a high point. Sure, there was a lot of bad happening now. But he had been nothing but good.

Brett pulled her to him, placing a kiss on her stomach. He drew his tongue up her abdomen. He pulled the cup of her bra back, exposing her breast. Brett ran his teeth over her nipple, and she bit her lip to stifle a cry of pleasure and pain.

He worked her zipper down lower before running his finger inside of her panties. Eva spread her knees farther, giving him full access to her body. He slid a finger inside of her. With his thumb, he rubbed the top of her sex. His touch ignited a flame in her belly, until she burned with a need to have him inside of her.

The orgasm claimed her. Her fingers tingled, and her skin felt too tight. She sucked in a breath, just a hiss of sound. Even that was too much. She buried her face in his hair. She held him and shuddered as the last spasms left her body.

Cradling the back of her head, he placed his mouth next to her ear and whispered, "Take off your clothes."

His hot breath washed over her, and yet gooseflesh rose on her arms.

She wanted to feel him again, skin to skin.

Eva kicked off her shoe, careful not to make a sound. She pulled the zipper down the rest of the way before shimmying out of her flight suit. The cool evening air caressed her skin.

Brett knelt next to her. He slowly traced her body with his fingertips. Shoulder, belly, hip and thigh.

She shivered in anticipation and lay back on the sandy ground.

"So beautiful," he whispered, he slipped his finger inside of her.

She wanted to moan. To scream with pleasure. Biting the inside of her lip, she ran her fingers through his hair.

Brett slipped another finger inside of her, filling her completely. He kissed the top of her sex, sucking and licking.

A bolt of pleasure electrified her body. She bucked, lifting her hips, and brought his mouth closer still. Although his kisses and touches could never be deep enough.

She felt her next orgasm building, a swelling that started in her middle and grew as it traveled through her body. But she wanted more. She wanted him inside of her when she came. Eva tugged on his shoulders.

Brett looked up from between her thighs. The sight left her lightheaded.

"Come here." She mouthed the words. "I want you."

Brett slid up the length of her body, kissing her as he went. Her pelvis. Her stomach. Her chest. Her breasts. He rested on top of her, his face only inches from her own. God, he was gorgeous. The muscles of his chest and shoulders were defined. The hard planes of his face were all the sharper in the shadows.

She kissed him again, deeper than before. The taste

of her own pleasure lingered on his tongue. "Take me," she said, her words nothing more than a whisper on the wind.

Brett unzipped his own flight suit, stripping it down past his ass. She wrapped her legs around his waist. She was so wet that he entered her in one stroke.

They moved together. In the moment, there was nothing beyond her and Brett. He pumped his hips, driving into her harder and faster. She could feel an orgasm rising inside of her, the swell of a wave coming in fast and strong. Then, the surf crashed over her.

She wanted to cry out as the orgasm pulled her under and left her breathless. Pressing her mouth to his shoulder, she stifled her cries.

Brett drove into her harder. Faster. His breathing was harsh and ragged. He came, collapsing on top of her. He kissed her gently. The silence and the kiss communicated more than words ever would.

She stripped all the way out of her flight suit. After all, it was still wet and needed time to dry. It didn't bother Eva that they couldn't speak. She wasn't sure what she would say now anyway.

She sat on the ground; Brett took up a spot next to her. Their shoulders touched. The lovemaking left her spent. It felt as if she were no longer made of bones and muscles, but was something soft and malleable. Her brain had turned to mush as well, and her eyelids were heavy. Sleep was creeping toward her again from all sides.

She realized she had the luxury of feeling this way because she could trust Brett.

"You look tired," he said, his voice soft.

"I feel tired."

"Rest," he encouraged. "I'll keep watch. But I think we're safe tonight."

She nodded and placed a kiss on his cheek. In the moment, she felt safe and protected. Resting her head on his shoulder, Eva finally closed her eyes and slept.

Ryan and Isaac were once again in the helicopter piloted by Farrah. They'd been forced to stay grounded because of an unexpected storm, but now, they were on the move again. A team from the state police and the coroner's office had taken charge of the wreckage; there was nothing more they could do at the site.

"I've done a bit of math," said Farrah into her mic. "We're flying to the last place that the air ambulance showed up on radar. From there, I'll head south. Hopefully, we'll find a clue as to where the chopper went down—and if there are any other survivors."

"All eyes peeled on the ground and in the river," Isaac said, his tone terse.

The helicopter was equipped with a spotlight that swept back and forth over the ground.

Ryan sat on the left side, peering out the window. He wasn't sure what they hoped to find. After all, it was dark. Still, he could see enough to know that for miles, there was nothing other than rocks and dirt and the occasional scraggily tree or scrubby bush.

Then he saw a flash of light reflected off metal.

"Farrah, ahead and to the left," Ryan said. "I saw something."

"Roger that," she said. She eased the helicopter to the left and lowered their altitude.

He held his breath and stared out the window. A black shape lay in the middle of a small valley. "That's it," he said, tapping his finger on the window. "Do you see it?"

"I see it," said Farrah.

"Me, too," said Isaac, leaning over from his seat. "Now to find out what it is."

"On it," she said.

As soon as the skids touched the ground, Ryan unbuckled his harness and removed his headset. Isaac already had the cargo door open. Ryan jumped out of the aircraft first, ducking low to avoid the downdraft. As he ran, he pulled a flashlight from a backpack he had slung over one shoulder. He shone the beam into the darkness.

Isaac was right behind him with his own flashlight.

From five yards out, Ryan could tell that it was the tail rotor and rear section of a helicopter. He stopped and swept the flashlight beam over the ground, searching for other clues.

A stretcher lay on its side, the legs and undercarriage visible. He couldn't tell if anyone was on the stretcher.

Nearby, rocks were arranged in a pile.

"Interesting," Isaac said, staring at the rocks. "Almost like a memorial."

Ryan sucked in a breath. "But for who—or how many? And who survived the crash to make the memorial?"

"Right now," Isaac said, "all we know for sure is that the stretcher has to be Decker's."

Ryan nodded, then looked around slowly. "And he's nowhere to be seen."

Isaac removed his firearm from the holster on his hip. Holding the gun with one hand and the flashlight in the other, he kept the barrel and the beam pointed toward the ground. "Let's check it, but be careful."

Ryan let Isaac take point—after all, he was the one with the gun. But the stretcher was eerily still. If Decker was still handcuffed to the railing, he hadn't survived the crash. For a moment, he recalled their childhood. Both had been hungry for glory and riches. In a way, they were kindred spirits. But in those days, Decker still had a soul.

How would Ryan feel to see the corpse of a man he once loved like a brother but now loathed? He rounded the stretcher and stopped short.

Standing at his side, Isaac cursed and slipped his gun back into the holster.

The sheets were empty. One of the railings was missing. A set of handcuffs lay on the ground.

In that moment, Ryan knew exactly what had happened. But still, he needed proof. He shone the flashlight beam at the pile of rocks. A shiver ran through him. "Not just a memorial. A *grave*."

"I'm thinking you're right," Isaac said.

They spent a few minutes removing the rocks. Like Ryan had predicted, it was a grave. But he didn't recognize the man who'd been buried.

"Do you know this guy?" Ryan asked.

"Yeah," said Isaac. "It's Augustin Herrera, US marshal."

"Another thing we know for sure," Ryan said, "is that Decker sure didn't bury the marshal."

Isaac nodded. "Right. Let's replace the stones."

They got it done, covering the dead man once more. Farrah would radio in that another body had been found, and the US marshal would be taken away in a body bag. Until then, there was no reason to disturb his resting place.

Dusting his hands on the seat of his jeans, Ryan said, "There were seven people on that helicopter, right? So far, we've found four bodies. It means that Decker's either dead, or he survived and took off. It also means that either the pilot, the nurse or both survived. One of those two buried the marshal." He paused a moment before adding, "We have to get to the other survivors before they become Decker's next victims."

Chapter 13

Every step sent a shock wave of pain and nausea roiling through Decker's body. A cold sweat coated his flesh like a second slimy skin. He climbed to the top of a hill and scanned the dark terrain.

It was filled with hills and rocky outcroppings that all looked like each other. But his eyes had gotten used to the dark, and his ears had become accustomed to the silence. He waited, watching and listening. There was no movement. No far-off sounds of voices.

He needed the meds in the kit. He'd been following the nurse and the pilot for miles. But then the effing storm had come out of nowhere, and he lost their trail.

He tried to recall the last several hours. Each time an idea came to him, his head felt like it was being split in two by a cleaver. His mouth hurt. His feet were sore. He wished like hell that he'd stolen the marshal's shirt. The baggy windbreaker had rubbed his shoulders and pits raw.

If he were a sensible man, he'd ignore the pain and the withdrawal symptoms and just get his butt to Mexico. All he needed was the phone to call Seraphim.

What the hell was wrong with him? Relying on pills

was weakness in his mind. Yet, here he was—weak, sick and lost.

Indecision rooted him to the spot. What was his next best plan? He could keep walking and make it—somehow—to Mexico. Or he could turn around and try to find the med kit. He'd have to take it from the pilot and the nurse, but hey, he was the one with the gun. That pleasant thought almost lessened the pain shooting up and down his arms and legs.

He looked over his shoulder. The terrain was much as what lay before him. He couldn't think about going back when he'd already made it this far.

Wind blew along the spine of the hill, cutting through the thin jacket. Decker started to shake with the cold. Wrapping his arms around his chest, he tried to conserve his heat and contain the shivers. He did neither. His stomach revolted.

Dropping to his hands and knees, he vomited acidic bile onto the dirt. He was too exhausted to stand, too exhausted to move. He rolled onto his back, the gun digging into his flesh. He didn't mind—at least the pain was real.

Lying there on the top of a hill, he stared at the night sky and the endless stars.

Decker wasn't a complex man. He understood two things—dominance and death. But as he lay on his back, he wondered if there was more to life than taking what he wanted. For the first time in years, he wondered if things would have been different—if he would have been different—if Anastasia hadn't left him when she did.

His stomach roiled again. Decker rolled to his side

as vomit trickled from his mouth. He wanted to scoot away from the puddle of barf, but he was too tired. His feet and legs were numb. Oblivion was coming to claim him, and he welcomed the void.

He wouldn't get much farther without something to stop the pain.

He had to find the med kit in the morning. If it meant killing the pilot and the nurse, so be it. As consciousness finally faded, he brought Ana's face to mind and whispered, "Someday soon, I'll find you."

Ryan glanced at his smartwatch: 3:47 a.m. He hadn't slept since the night before. But it didn't matter. He wouldn't be able to rest until Decker Newcombe had been found and captured.

A mobile command center had been set up near the crash site. Aside from Ryan and Isaac, Jason Jones was there with a cadre of FBI agents. A coroner had been flown in to collect the body of US Marshal Augustin Herrera. There was also a representative from the Marshals Service, Maria Reyes, the supervisor from the San Antonio office. The group also had two Texas Rangers and an agent from the ATF. Mooky Parsons, the local sheriff, rounded out the team.

Lights on tall poles had been set up around the perimeter.

The alphabet soup of law enforcement left Ryan jittery. Not long ago, all these people had been out looking for him, as well. Sure, he'd changed teams and was even working for Texas Law now. But his distrust and dislike of the police was like a splinter that had been driven in deep. It bothered him when touched and was damn near impossible to get rid of or ignore.

It was a supreme irony that he was dating the local undersheriff. But Kathryn Glass was the exception to nearly every rule he'd created for his life.

The coroner, Sheila Garcia, was clad in full PPE with a mask, surgical cap and latex gloves. Approaching Maria, she held a small clear, plastic bag. "Here are the personal effects we found on the body."

Ryan stood more than five yards away, but he could see that there wasn't much beyond a wallet and a few photos.

"This is it?" asked Maria. "What about his clothes? His gun? His phone?"

"For now," said the coroner, "I'm leaving the deceased in his T-shirt and underwear for dignity's sake. But everything else is gone."

"Gone," the marshal echoed, as if the word was foreign to her. She shook her head slowly and looked at Jason. "Poor Auggie." And then, "We have to assume that Decker Newcombe stole all his belongings."

Before he could think better of it, Ryan said, "That's not true."

All eyes turned to Ryan. He hated having so many cops stare at him. In the past, it had never ended well.

"Excuse me?" Maria said. "What did you say?"

Well, he'd opened his big mouth already. There was no turning back. "Decker wouldn't take the phone."

She snorted a laugh. "How would you know?"

"Because I know him."

Isaac said, "Ryan's with Texas Law now. But he used

to be Decker's business manager and friend. He knows him better than anyone."

"Oh." Maria looked at Ryan, sizing him up from the top of his head to the toe of his boots. Her face was pinched like she'd tasted something sour. "I heard about you. You're the one who got a sweetheart of a deal."

Jason said, "He's also the reason Decker was in custody in the first place. You want to find the guy who killed your agent, we do, too. And like it or not, Ryan's the person we need to find the killer."

In a day that had been full of surprises, Special Agent Jones standing up for him was one hell of a shock. Ryan wasn't used to praise. He couldn't help it and stood a little taller.

The marshal sniffed. "If you're such a specialist, what do you know about Decker?"

"He didn't take Herrera's phone for starters," Ryan insisted. "He'd know it could be used to track him."

"What else?"

"He definitely didn't bury your guy, either. It's not his style."

"What does all of that mean?" Maria asked.

"It means that there are other survivors of the crash. They took time to bury the body, and they're the ones who have the phone."

"That would make sense," said Jason. "The pilot and nurse haven't been found."

The marshal nodded slowly. "The good news is, assuming there's power, we can track the phone."

"It might not bring us to Decker, but it'll do some

good," Ryan said, surprised that he was genuinely glad to help someone in need.

"Let me make a call." A large metal satellite phone was hooked on Maria's belt next to her firearm. She pulled it free and walked outside the ring of lights. The night was still and silent, and it was impossible to miss the tones as she pressed the sat phone's keypad.

After a moment, she said, "Sorry to call so late— or maybe it's early—but I need a location on Herrera's phone." She paused. "There's no cellular coverage here, you'll have to call me back at this number with coordinates." Another pause. "Thanks. I appreciate it."

She walked back to the group. "I assume you all heard that?" Without waiting for an answer, she continued, "It'll take some time, but we can find the phone—and whoever's got it." Maria turned to Ryan. "Now, I have to ask you an important question. Where is the subject now?"

After Jason had built him up as an expert on everything Decker Newcombe, it pained Ryan to admit the truth. "Honestly?" he said. "I have no idea."

Even before he pried his lids open, Decker's eyes hurt. His teeth ached from clenching his jaw all night. His mouth was dry, his tongue thick. He shivered and wrapped the jacket tighter around his torso. He didn't know how he'd survived the night without his meds, but somehow he had.

It reminded him of the old joke. He was only alive because heaven didn't want him, and hell was afraid he'd take over.

After wiping grit from his eyes, Decker looked at the sky. It was still black, but only a few stars were still visible. He'd slept for hours and somehow felt worse for the rest.

As he sat up, a wave of nausea crashed over him. He started to heave and rolled onto all fours. Nothing came up. He was so thirsty—for water and meds both—that it felt like a knife in his gut. There was no way he'd make it to Mexico without something for the cravings.

The gun he'd shoved into his waistband pulled his pants lower. Tightening his belt, Decker reviewed what he knew.

Yesterday evening, he had been following the pilot and the nurse until he lost them in the storm. If he wanted to find them again, he had to double back. Yet, he knew that getting the med kit wasn't just something he wanted. It was something he needed.

He pushed to standing. His vision blurred, and the ground beneath his feet rocked like a boat on the ocean. It was the damned addiction to the meds, he knew. Still, he thought he might retch again. Or he would if he had anything left in his stomach.

Inhaling deeply, he placed one foot in front of the other.

Focus, dammit. Stay sharp.

But he couldn't concentrate. Every joint felt as if it were being crushed. His eyes ached too much to scan the horizon or study the ground for clues.

Then he heard it. A sound—something had clattered. He stopped walking and listened.

Silence.

Was it them? The pilot and the nurse? He knew the general direction the sound had come from. Maybe he'd get lucky. He pulled the gun from the small of his back and gripped the handle with both hands. Carefully, he crept along the ridgeline. His steps were slow. His footfalls crunched on the gravel and hard-packed earth.

Now he heard a skittering sound. It stopped suddenly—purposefully.

He retreated several steps, trying to find the spot where he heard the noise.

The sounds had come from his left, farther up the hill. From where he stood, he could see a narrow gap in the rocks. There was a flash of blue against a white background and a red cross. It was one of the flight suits. Someone was barely visible at the edge of the opening. Keeping guard.

He removed the magazine from his gun and counted the bullets. Five rounds left. He reinserted the clip and lined the sight up with the red cross. His hands shook. His eyes stung as his vision wavered and turned the target fuzzy.

Decker didn't like his chances of hitting anything. He didn't like the idea of wasting any more bullets, either. If he was going to get the med kit, he had to get close.

Quietly, he climbed the hill. From there, he could look down and see everything. The pilot lay on his side, sleeping. He snored. Beside him, the nurse kept watch.

There was no way he could sneak past the nurse. Nor could he shoot them both, not with his withdrawal shakes.

In short, he didn't have a plan.

Yet, Decker did have certain things on his side—like time and patience. He settled behind a boulder. From there, he could watch and wait, finding the perfect time to strike.

Eva sat at the edge of the cave and watched as the sun crested over the horizon. A minute ago, a raccoon had rushed past her and knocked over the med kit, making it spin a bit. She'd hurried to silence the noise. Not just because Brett was sleeping and had barely gotten a couple of hours in. But because Decker Newcombe could be out there.

She hoped he'd moved on, giving up on trying to kill them to get as far away as possible. Otherwise, he risked getting recaptured.

But Decker was an irrational serial killer. She couldn't count on him being reasonable, even about his own life.

She let herself watch the sunrise. For a moment, it was just a line of gold, and then it erupted into light. The day was going to be brutally hot. Even at this early hour, the temperatures had started to rise. She knew they shouldn't walk in the hottest part of the day, which meant that they had to take advantage of the light now.

After she and Brett had made love, she'd slept for several hours. Brett, gallant guy that he was, would've let her continue to sleep. But in the middle of the night, she'd awakened. She'd insisted that it was her turn to keep watch. Brett must've been exhausted because he agreed to let her stay up.

Now, she hated to wake him.

Brett lay on his back. His cheeks and chin were covered in stubble. She ran a finger over his chin.

He opened his eyes slowly.

"Hey," she said as his gaze rested on her face.

"Hey," he echoed. He glanced at the watch on his wrist. He pressed the crown on the side once and then, once more. "Damned battery" he said, his voice hoarse. "Any idea what time it is?"

"It's daybreak. So maybe five in the morning," she guessed. "How're you feeling?"

Sitting up, he scrubbed his face with both hands. "Better," he said. "Thanks for letting me sleep. We should probably get going."

"Agreed," said Eva. "But we should eat something first." They still had two days' worth of rations left.

"Let's eat while we walk." He stood. "But first, you'll have to excuse me. Nature calls."

Brett's absence gave her time to get ready for a day filled with walking. After straightening one sock, she slipped on a sneaker. As she reached for the air cast, a shadow—head, shoulders, arms—stretched out on the floor of the cave.

"That was fast," she said, turning.

A man stood at the cave's entrance. The sun shone on him from behind and obscured his features. But even without seeing his face, she knew the man wasn't Brett.

Decker Newcombe stepped forward into the cave. His icy blue eyes were dull. His hair hung around his shoulders. The stink of infection and vomit surrounded him like a fog. Holding a gun, Decker aimed the barrel at her chest.

She tried to scream, but all she could manage was a croak. "What do you want?"

"The medical kit. Give it to me."

Eva reached for the kit and held it up. "Take it."

"Push it here."

She set it back on the ground and shoved it toward the killer.

He knelt and lifted it by the handle. With his eyes on her, and the barrel aimed at Eva's head, he tucked the box into his chest. With his thumb, he unlocked the latch and flipped the lid open. Casting his gaze to the box, he shoved the contents around. He looked back at her; his gaze was filled with fury and pain. She'd seen that look more than once in the ER.

He asked, "Where's the good stuff?"

"Good stuff?" she repeated, though she could guess what he was looking for. "You want pain meds?"

"Yeah, and none of that over-the-counter crap."

"San Antonio Medical Center has a policy not to carry narcotics in ambulances," she said. Years ago, several EMTs had been robbed for the drugs they carried. "We don't take anything strong out of the hospital. Everything you were prescribed was separate from this. I don't know where those meds went but I guess they were lost in the crash." She paused, not sure why she was trying to reason with a killer. Still, she was nurse and she had to try. "But you were hurt in the crash… I can help you."

She didn't want to tend to a killer, but she took her oath to help seriously.

"I didn't get some other damn injury," he said. "What

I need are drugs. And it's all your fault. If the hospital hadn't pumped me full of crap, I wouldn't need it now."

Had Decker become addicted to pain meds? It happened so often that she wasn't surprised. "There are things you can take to help with the cravings." With her hands lifted, she rose to her feet. "Let me show you."

"You're the nurse," he said. "Eva, right?"

"That's right." Even she heard the tremor in her voice.

She'd been in tough situations before over the years. The only way to survive was to keep her cool. But this man was much worse than a belligerent patient who'd come to the emergency department. She didn't have the support of other nurses or doctors or hospital security. Decker Newcombe was a serial killer, and she was alone. Even if she treated him to overcome his craving, she couldn't expect him to be thankful. Hell, she shouldn't expect to survive.

Still, the med kit contained an opioid receptor antagonist, naloxone, a drug that would minimize Decker's withdrawals. Swallowing her fear, she said, "I can help you, if you let me."

"Well, that's so kind of you to offer. Now get up, Nurse Eva." He pressed the gun into the top of her head. The iron was cold, and the barrel dug a groove into her skin over her skull. "You're coming with me."

Chapter 14

Brett stood on a ridge and looked in every direction. The sky was a soft shade of blue and the sun had yet to crest over the horizon. In this light, the red rocks were a deep shade of ocher. The few plants hardy enough to grow in this area of the desert were brown at the edges. But the interstate was out there, somewhere. He knew where it was.

There were several hills between where he stood and where they needed to be. To find the road, they'd have to traverse miles of grueling terrain. They had food but hadn't saved any of the rainwater. The sun and the heat would be their worst enemies—that was if they could avoid Decker Newcombe altogether.

Now that he had his bearings, Brett walked back to the cave. He stopped at the entrance and froze. Eva was gone. The med kit was gone.

Two sets of footprints were impressed in the sand.

One set had to belong to Decker. Had the killer been watching and waiting? And more important, where were they now? Brett hadn't been gone long—a few minutes, no more. They couldn't have gone far.

He followed the set of prints to a bare rock ledge.

Without the sandy dirt, there were no more footprints. Like a magician's trick, there the trail was gone. He walked to the edge, shading his eyes to scan the horizon. There were rocks and hills and brush. But no sign of Eva or Decker.

He had to get her back. But how?

A scream ripped through the silent morning. It echoed off the hills, seeming to come from everywhere. He ran, not even sure if he was going the correct direction.

A root snaked along the ground. He didn't see it until it was too late. His toe caught, and he fell, skidding along the rocks. Ignoring the pain in his knees and the pinpricks of blood that filled his palms, he pushed to his feet and started to run.

"Eva!" he yelled. "Can you hear me? Where are you?"

"Brett!" she screamed.

The one word was all he needed to find the right direction. Swerving to the left, he ran up a steep hill. Stones came loose under his feet, rolling down behind him. Clawing his way to the top, he reached the summit.

At the edge of a cliff stood Eva. Her eyes were wide with fear. Decker clutched her from behind. One of the killer's arms was wrapped around her neck. In the other hand, he held a gun. The barrel was pointed at Brett's chest.

"Stay where you are, flyboy."

"Are you okay, Eva?" Of course, she wasn't. "Did he hurt you?"

"I'm fine," she said. "You have to get out of here."

"I'm not going anywhere without you." And then, to

Decker, Brett said, "Let her go and take me." He took a step forward.

"I told you to stay where you are. You move again, and I'll shoot you both."

Brett lifted his hands in surrender. But so long as he drew breath, he wasn't about to let Decker hurt Eva. He just didn't know how he was supposed to fight back when the killer had a gun—and Eva was his hostage.

"You don't have to do this," Brett said, trying to be reasonable. "You can let her go. We won't follow you. We can't tell the authorities where you've gone."

"I don't care about you," said Decker. "All I want is the meds and the nurse to make sure I get well."

"You aren't taking her." Brett's voice was clear and confident. It was in total contrast to the fear that gnawed at his belly.

"I don't know that you're in any position to make demands." Decker turned the barrel, pressing the gun into the side of Eva's head. "You take another step, and I'll shoot."

"You aren't going to kill her." Brett was certain that Decker needed—or maybe wanted—Eva alive. Then to her, he said, "It'll be okay. I'm here. I'll keep you safe."

She nodded as if she believed him.

He had to keep his promise, but how?

Decker snorted. "You think I got a problem murdering someone? Flyboy, you don't know who you're dealing with."

"You aren't going to kill her," he said, "because you need her."

"Actually," said Decker, "you're right."

Pointing the gun at Brett, he pulled the trigger.

A flash of fire erupted from the muzzle. A boom like a thunderclap rolled across the desert, and white-hot pain knocked Brett down. The rocky ground bit into his flesh. Blood trickled down the side of his sleeve. Carefully, he touched the top of his arm. The raw flesh stung. Damn. He had no idea how bad the injury was, but blood wasn't gushing. That was a good sign.

"Oh my God, you shot him!" Eva screamed. "You really shot him!"

Without thinking, Brett launched himself at Decker. The killer still had the gun in his hand, but Brett had a split second to get Eva away from him.

Just like he'd been taught in high school football practice, he wrapped his arms around Eva's torso and pulled her away. "Run, Eva, and don't look back!" He hoped like hell that she would be fast enough to escape. If she was going to get away, he had to keep Decker from going after her.

It had been years since he'd been given any instruction on hand-to-hand combat. Even then, his lessons had been perfunctory. But he remembered enough.

Brett kicked the man's knee—hard. Decker folded like a house of cards on a windy day and crumpled, the gun dropping to the ground.

"You son of a bitch." Spittle flew from Decker's mouth. He scrambled to his feet and lunged forward, slamming his head into Brett's middle. All the air left his body in a single gust, leaving him dazed and flat on his back. The killer was on top of him, wrapping his hands around Brett's throat and pinning him to the ground. "I'll kill you for that."

Decker's fingers dug into Brett's flesh. Brett slammed his fists into the other man's arm, trying to break his hold. It did no good. Blackness crept in from the sides, and every part of his body burned, screaming for air.

"Let him go, Decker." Eva stood at his side with the gun in her hand.

Decker loosened his grip.

Gulping down breaths and coughing, Brett rolled to his knees.

"What do you think you're going to do with that gun, Eva?" Decker asked.

"I should shoot you," she said, "for everything you've done."

"But you won't," said Decker. "Remember, you were going to help me. That's the kind of person you are. Helpful. Compassionate."

"Maybe I was," she said, "but that was before you took me as a hostage and tried to kill Brett."

Rising to his feet, Brett rubbed his throat, not sure if he could speak. "Give me the gun, Eva." His voice was hoarse as each word scraped over his bruised larynx. "You don't want to kill Decker."

"And you do?"

She touched on a difficult question. Just like the proverbial dog that finally caught the car, Brett didn't know what to do now that the killer was held at gunpoint. Of course, he hated the idea of shooting an unarmed man. But even though Decker didn't have a weapon, he was still dangerous and deadly. They couldn't let him go. Nor could they keep him as a prisoner.

Like she'd been reading his mind, Eva asked another question. "What are we going to do now?"

Brett turned to meet her eyes. Their gazes locked and held.

An instant was all the time that Decker needed. He lunged at Eva, grabbing her around the middle. Unprepared, she fired the gun, sending a bullet into the sky.

Holding on to her, Decker kept going. He grabbed the gun and shoved her off the cliff.

Brett rushed forward, but he wasn't fast enough. By the time he got to where she'd stood, Eva was gone. Ten feet below, she lay on a rock ledge. She didn't move. He couldn't even tell if she breathed.

He turned to Decker. "You did this." His voice was stronger than he could believe.

Decker pointed the gun at him. "You should've let me take her. At least she'd be alive."

Enraged, Brett was about to lunge for Decker when a twig snapped nearby.

Decker shot wildly in that direction, but it was just a critter of some kind. The distraction gave Brett the chance to run behind an outcropping of rocks. He glanced out from behind it. Decker had decided his odds weren't good, even with the gun, and was running away with the med kit.

For an instant, Brett was rooted to the ground. Did he chase after the killer or climb down to Eva?

Well, when he thought about it that way, there really wasn't a choice at all.

Drawing in a deep breath, he turned to lower himself over the edge of the cliff. His legs dangled uselessly into the void for a moment, then his feet connected with the side of the mountain. Placing one foot, then the other on a small, narrow ledge, Brett eased down the side of the cliff. He could just make out a series of cracks in the rock wall that might let him reach the shelf where Eva lay.

He scooted his feet along the ledge until it ended, then stretched one leg out to reach his next toehold. But when his toe hit, the rock crumbled away.

Suddenly weightless, he could feel himself falling.

Throwing himself forward, Brett clung to the wall of stone. His heart hammered in his chest. Sweat streamed from his hairline, burning his eyes. He blinked hard.

Drawing in a deep breath, he looked down at Eva.

She hadn't moved.

Was she even alive?

He had to ignore all the doubt. He wouldn't survive if he didn't focus. Shifting his foot out to a farther hold, he took a breath and started to climb down. When he only had a few feet left between him and Eva, he jumped.

The landing sent a shock wave through his feet, knees and hips.

Kneeling next to Eva, he watched her chest rise and fall. Thank God. She was still breathing. He touched her shoulder. "Eva? Can you hear me?"

She didn't stir.

By 6:00 a.m., there had been no new intel. It left the law enforcement officers with nothing to do but hurry up and wait.

Ryan hated the inactivity.

He heard a sharp trill at the same instant Maria reached for the satellite phone hooked to her belt. "What have you got for me?" she asked into the phone. A moment later, she yelled, "We've got coordinates for Augustin's phone! Someone get me a map."

"I have one." Jason spread a topographical map on a folding table set up under one of the lights.

"I need a pen," Maria said.

Ryan removed a pen that had been tucked into a side pocket on his cargo pants. "Here you go."

Maria took it, nodding her thanks.

"Go ahead," she said to the person on the other end of the call. The marshal repeated a series of numbers, scribbling them onto the margins of the map. Finally, she said, "Thanks. You've been a lifesaver." She ended the call. Maria circled a point on the map. "This is where the phone is located."

"That's less than five miles from here," Jason said at a glance. "Farrah, can you fly to that point?"

"Fly? Yes. Land? No." She pressed her finger onto the map. The contour lines were close together, denoting a steep slope. "There's no flat surface. But if I get into the sky, I can conduct a grid search."

"A team should head in that direction on foot," Ryan spoke up. "If Farrah finds anything, she can let the ground team know."

Farrah said, "I'd want someone in the chopper with me. There's no way I can fly and manage a thorough search at the same time."

"I'll go up in the helicopter," Jason said. "I can take some of my agents with me."

Maria said, "I've got the sat phone and the only way to make contact from the ground. I'll lead the team that goes in on foot."

"Ryan and I will come with you," said Isaac.

"I'd appreciate that," she said.

With a plan in place, everyone started to move. Before Ryan took a step, Maria placed her hand on his arm. "You got a minute?"

"I guess."

"I know I busted your balls earlier, but you've had some good ideas. I'm not usually wrong, but it seems like I misjudged you. In my book, you're all right."

It wasn't exactly an apology. It wasn't exactly a compliment, either. But it didn't matter, Ryan would take it. "Thanks," he said. "That's nice of you."

"Don't get all mushy." Maria folded up the map and slid it into a pants pocket. "And if you fall behind, I'm not waiting around."

Isaac approached with two backpacks. He handed one to Ryan. "Are we ready?"

Maria picked up a backpack that was sitting on the ground. "I'm ready—and I'm not waiting for you, either."

Isaac placed his hand on Ryan's shoulder, holding him back. "What was all that about?"

"It seems like Maria Reyes doesn't hate me as much as she did before," Ryan said, partly joking.

Resting the backpack on the table, he examined its contents: a water bottle, a first aid kit, a space blanket, a compass. At the bottom of the bag was a 9mm Beretta 92 tucked inside a holster. He loosened the belt on his jeans, wove it through the holster and fastened his belt again.

"You ready?" Isaac asked. "Because I don't think that the marshal is kidding about leaving us behind."

But what concerned Ryan the most was that Decker Newcombe was still out there. If the two men ever met again, one of them wouldn't come back alive.

Decker sat in the shade of a large boulder and waited. It was the perfect place to ambush the pilot—apparently the guy's name was Brett—if he came after him. But honestly, Decker didn't think he would.

After five minutes, he stopped looking. Resting against the rock, he unlocked the med kit. His hands shook. He wanted pain meds, but now he knew that he needed something else.

He rifled through the contents, looking for the naloxone that Eva had mentioned. He found it, read the dosing instructions and inserted the tip of the nasal spray into a nostril.

Inhaling sharply, he squeezed the dispenser.

The spray filled his sinuses with cold droplets. He inhaled again until his lungs filled.

He exhaled. There was no relief. His head still throbbed. His joints still ached. His hands still shook.

But maybe the headache wasn't as bad. His body still hurt, but within a few minutes the pain began to lessen. For the first time in weeks, he could concentrate.

The first thing that came to mind was his enemy: Ryan Steele. If it hadn't been for that traitor, Decker's name would already be added to the history books. Generations from now, people would still know of his crime. His name would be the one that children feared in the middle of the night.

But Ryan had rescued his victim in the middle of the act. Not only had Decker been stopped, but he'd also been beaten, shot and humiliated. God, he could only imagine the memes that were circulating.

And then there was Ana. Lying, kid-withholding Ana. *I'm coming for you*, he thought.

And my son.

Decker tucked the med kit under his arm and stood. His stomach grumbled, and his mouth was dry. But his bones no longer ached. His flesh no longer itched.

He didn't know how many more doses he might need to overcome his cravings. But now, maybe he'd be able to make it to Mexico. Then, he'd retrieve his phone. He'd deal with Ana. Oh, yes. He'd make sure she knew what it felt like to lose a child. She'd feel the same pain he had when she disappeared, leaving nothing behind. And it had been because she was pregnant? The fact that she didn't want him to be a father hurt worse than the rejection.

Once he had his son, Decker would rebuild his reputation. He'd go from being the butt of jokes to the most terrifying person who ever lived.

Eva hung in the space between dreams and wakefulness. Her head hurt. Her back ached. Her shoulder was sore. Her eyes were swollen, and her tongue was thick.

She felt as if she were submerged, swimming deep in

the waters of the Gulf of Mexico. An icy hand was keeping her underwater. She wanted to breathe but couldn't.

From the shore, someone called her name.

She tried to answer, but water filled her mouth. She started to cough.

Then a set of strong hands pulled her from the depths, and she opened her eyes. A man knelt next to her. The sun shone on him from behind, hiding his features in the shadows. And still, he was familiar. She screwed her eyes shut.

"Eva," the man said. She recognized his voice. He was the one who'd been calling to her from the beach. "Can you hear me?"

She tried to speak, but all that came out was a moan.

"Are you hurt? You took quite a fall."

How could she have fallen? Just a minute ago, she was in the ocean.

Then, she remembered everything. The helicopter crash. The storms. Taking refuge in a cave. Decker Newcombe, sick with withdrawal symptoms. He'd thrown her over a cliff.

And finally, she remembered him.

"Brett," she whispered. "Where am I?"

"You hit a ledge on your way down. Lucky for you. The rest of the fall…" His words trailed off. "Well, let's just say that falling all the way to the bottom of the ravine would've been bad. Very bad."

Honestly, everything ached. She wiggled her toes. Bent her knees. Lifted both arms. There were no sharp pains. "I think I'm okay."

"Can you sit?"

"Help me up."

Brett placed one hand on her shoulder and the other on her elbow. He pushed from the back and pulled from the front. "I'll help. Let me know if it's too much, and we'll stop." His touch was soothing, his words reassuring.

She engaged her core and lifted her head and shoulders. Reaching for her bent knees, she pulled herself to sitting. The exertion left her winded. She wheezed, "I'm okay."

"Take your time." Brett rubbed her shoulder. "Decker has the med kit. He's not coming back for us."

She nodded. "I just want to get out of here."

"Do you think you can stand? We need to climb that thing." He nodded toward a sheer rock wall that was almost a dozen feet high. She tried to swallow, but a hard knot was stuck in her throat. "And then, there's still miles of walking to find the interstate."

Thank goodness she'd put back on her air cast when she woke to take over the watch in the middle of the night. At that time, she redressed in her flight suit, as well. Putting on the boot had been an afterthought. Now, she was thankful she'd taken the time. Still, if finding civilization seemed difficult yesterday, today it felt impossible.

She just didn't have any other options.

Chapter 15

Eva stood. A bolt of pain shot through her ankle and wrapped around her leg. Her eyes watered. She cursed and stumbled. God, it felt good to be in his arms.

Brett caught her around the waist and kept her from toppling over. "What is it?" he asked.

"It's my damned ankle." Her jaw was tight, her teeth clenched.

"Is it the same one that was injured yesterday?"

"Yeah, but now it's about one hundred times worse." She inhaled and exhaled, thinking only of her breath. The pain in her foot dulled to an ache. "Maybe it was just stiff," she said, although she knew she was truly injured. How was she supposed to hike to the highway now? "I'm going to try to stand on it again."

Brett loosened his grip on her waist. "I'm still here to keep you safe."

She liked the idea of having him next to her. But really, she didn't have the bandwidth to worry about her love life—or lack thereof. Not now, at least. She placed her foot on the ground, putting weight into the leg. Pain, like a poker shoved through her bone, left her breathless. "Dammit," she cursed.

"It's okay," he said, "I've got you."

"How am I supposed to walk to the interstate now?" Even she heard the despair in her voice. "I can barely stand."

Brett touched her chin with a finger, lifting her gaze to meet his. "I don't know what we'll do once we make it off of this ledge, but I do know that we can't stay here."

Eva stared at the wall of rock. It would be a hard climb under the best circumstances. And frankly, she wasn't at her best. "How?"

Brett exhaled—a sure sign that he was thinking. "I want you to hold on to my shoulders. With you on my back, I'll climb to the top. Then, we'll go to the cave where we were this morning. It's dry and will stay cool once it gets really hot. Plus, the food's still there—and the cell phones. Maybe we'll get lucky and have a signal."

"What if we don't?" Until now, Eva had been able to face each problem as it arose. Maybe it was the constant pain in her foot. Or maybe it was coming face-to-face with a killer. Or maybe it was the fact that she'd been thrown over a cliff. But now, the metallic taste of panic coated her tongue.

"I don't know." Brett shrugged. "I'm just as lost as you. Honestly, I'm making all this up as I go along."

"You're right," she said, surrendering. "But listen..."

"No, you listen," said Brett.

Was he really going to start a fight now? "Excuse me?"

"Do you hear that?"

Eva stood still. There was nothing, not even the sound

of the wind running along the spine of the mountain. "I don't hear anything," she began.

But that wasn't true. There was a faint *whomp, whomp, whomp.*

Her breath caught. "Is that a helicopter?"

"I think it is," said Brett, looking up at the sky. "I can't figure out where it's coming from, though."

Shading her eyes with her hand, she scanned the horizon. "There it is." She pointed at a black dot. "See?"

"Thank God." Brett waved his arm above his head. "Hey!" he yelled. "Over here!"

She doubted that the crew could hear them, but it didn't matter. Hope and excitement filled her chest until she thought she might burst. Waving her arms, she yelled, "Over here! Look this way, we're over here!"

The helicopter stayed on the horizon, never coming close. Finally, it disappeared from view, until even the noise of the rotors was too faint to hear.

Her eyes burned. Her throat was raw. Her ankle hurt worse than before. It would've been better if she'd never seen the helicopter and had the audacity to hope. "They didn't have a clue we were here."

"True," said Brett. "But they're searching for us, and they're close. I have no doubt they've laid out a grid and are going over each sector." He gave another exhale as he thought. "It's important that we get to the top. We'll be easier to spot in the open." His gaze traveled up the side of the hill. "You've got to hold on to my shoulders. I'm going to climb and pull us both out."

She'd seen every inch of his body. He was toned, muscular and fully male. But still, she would be a lot of weight to carry. "Are you sure? Maybe you could climb up and wave down the helicopter when it comes back."

"I'm not leaving you here."

"I'm not letting you kill yourself on my behalf."

He bent his elbow, tightening his biceps. The muscle was visible even under the sleeve of his flight suit. "You don't think I'm strong enough?"

"It's not a question of strength," she said. "It's a problem of balance. My weight is going to pull us both back and over."

"Everything's impossible until someone does it." He paused. "I'm willing to try. But if you aren't, then we'll think of something else."

She definitely wasn't convinced that this was the best plan. But she didn't know of any other options. "Okay," she said. "We'll do it."

Brett turned so she could grab on to his back. "Hold on," he said. "Don't lean back and don't let go."

After wrapping her arms around Brett's chest, she lifted her thighs up to his waist. "How's that?"

"Good," he said, wiping his hands on his legs. "Let's go." Brett reached up and worked both sets of fingers into a crack in the rock. He pulled up, using his legs to walk along the wall.

They rose from the ground one foot and then another. He rested his feet on a rock ledge. "That wasn't so hard," he said, his breath ragged.

"Keep your strength," Eva warned. "No talking."

"Got it," he said. Looking over his shoulder, he gave her a wide smile. Despite the circumstances and the pain in her ankle, a fluttering started in her middle.

He stopped on a ledge large enough for them to both stand. She unwrapped her legs and stood on the narrow outcropping. Leaning on the solid rock wall, she kept all her weight on her right foot. For a moment, she shook her hand and arms, which had gone numb from her tight hold. Blood rushed to her hands, filling her fingertips with sharp pinpricks. But it was a good pain.

"How are you holding up?" she asked.

Using the sleeve of his flight suit, Brett wiped sweat from his brow. "I figure I don't have any choice but to get us to the top now. We're too far up to go back. Let me know when you're ready."

The ledge offered them safety, but that was only temporary. "If you want to do the final climb, we can go now."

He turned so she could grab his shoulders, and she wrapped her legs once more around his waist. Once she was settled, Brett began the ascent.

They just had to make it to the top. A helicopter would spot them. Then, they'd be rescued. It was all so simple, it had to work.

At the same time, she knew each step was filled with risks and success wasn't guaranteed. But deep down in her gut, she knew that they'd make it. It was all because Brett was so damned optimistic. It was like his positive attitude was contagious and she'd caught the sunny disposition strain of the flu.

It was no wonder that she'd picked up something from him. From their first night together, when she couldn't wait to take him as her lover, they had definitely been much more than close. Or last night, where she needed the reassurance of his touch.

She held him tighter, resting her cheek on his back. With her cheek on his ribs, she could hear his breathing and the constant thumping of his heart. Both sounds were reassuring.

Yeah, the past few days had been a mess. But while holding on to Brett, she knew that there was no other person she wanted with her right now.

Too bad that by getting rescued, which was what she wanted, their time together would be over.

The muscles in Brett's arms burned with exertion. His hands were scraped, raw and aching. He wasn't sure if his back would ever be the same, but somehow, he'd done it. He'd scaled the cliff with Eva on his back.

She rolled off him, and he army-crawled forward, well away from the edge. For a moment, he lay on the dirt, breathing hard.

"You're amazing," she said. "I can't believe you pulled us all the way up that wall."

To be honest, he couldn't believe he had, either. Although quitting had never been an option. "What would you say if I told you that I never once reached the top of the rope in PE class?"

"I wouldn't believe you," she said. "And even if that's true, I think you deserve an A plus now."

He laughed. The muscles in his stomach contracted, and he groaned. Climbing up the cliff wall might have been the easy part. They still needed to traverse miles in this hostile climate, and Decker might still be lurking nearby.

Maybe he'd moved on by now, given that Decker had the med kit and no weapon. But Brett didn't put it past him to find creative ways to try to kill the only two witnesses who could report that he was alive.

The possibility that Brett might have to face the killer for a second time brought a chill to his soul.

"I'm just going to lie here for a minute," he said, "and catch my breath."

"Take all the time you need," said Eva. "You deserve a rest." She lay at his side and rested her head on his shoulder. "You did it." He turned his head to watch her. God, she was perfect. Beautiful. Smart. Brave. Dedicated and strong. Placing his lips on the top of her head, he whispered. "We did it together."

She rose up, resting on her elbow. "We make a pretty good team."

He ran his finger over her bottom lip. "We do."

She kissed the heel of his hand. His flesh was scraped and raw. "How are you?"

Honestly, every part of him hurt—especially his shoulder. "If my collarbone didn't burn with each breath, I'd almost forget that Decker shot me."

"It's the adrenaline," she said. "It numbs the pain for a while. I see it all the time in the emergency department. Too bad Decker took all our medical supplies." She smiled. It was better than seeing a sunrise after a stormy night. "I can kiss you and make it better."

"You think that'll work?" he asked, smiling at her in return.

"There's only one way to find out."

She bent to him, placing her lips on hers. Brett gripped the back of her head, pulling her to him, winding his fingers through her hair. He slipped his tongue into her mouth. This kiss was different from all the ones they'd shared before. He was no longer exploring her. Now, he knew Eva and this kiss was like coming home.

As much as he wanted to lay with her and hold her, staying here wasn't a good idea. He sat up, ending the embrace. They'd already survived a lot, but if they were really going to get home, they needed to take advantage of the cooler morning air.

Brett's pulse still raced. He could hear his heartbeat as it thumped. But wait. The sound didn't match the cadence of his pulse.

He pushed himself up to sitting and listened. There was nothing to hear. Had he been mistaken?

"What is it?" Eva brows were drawn together in concern. "Are you okay?"

"I thought I heard…" he didn't want to say what he thought it might be—what he hoped it was "…something," he concluded, noncommittal.

Shading her eyes with her hand, she glanced at the sky, then slowly stood and dusted the seat of her pants with her hands. "I don't see anything."

Disappointment, cold and heavy, dropped into his chest. Sure, he'd gotten Eva off the cliff's ledge, despite her wounded leg. Even he knew that the feat was damn near impossible. But could he rely on luck and fortitude to get them back to civilization?

Without a rescue helicopter, neither of them would

survive. Had he somehow created the sound that he most wanted to hear? The sweet, passionate kiss might have conjured it out of his determination to get her to safety. "Maybe I imagined it."

"I don't think so." She pointed to the horizon. "Listen."

He strained to hear, then stood, his abs and legs screaming in protest, and gazed at the sky.

And then he heard it again. The very faint whir of a chopper.

Suddenly, a black speck marred the cloudless blue sky. Even from where he stood, he knew it was a helicopter. All his aches and pains were forgotten.

"That's them." Excitement sent his pulse racing. "We have to get their attention."

"How are we supposed to do that?" she asked.

"We need something metal."

"Metal?" she repeated.

"Or something that's reflective."

"I know what we can use." She unzipped a breast pocket on her flight suit and pulled out her hospital ID. "It's not ideal." She held up the laminated ID. "But someone told me it does catch the light."

"None of this is ideal." Brett took the card, letting his fingertips linger on the back of her hand. "Let's hope this is enough."

Farrah had piloted too many search-and-rescue missions to count. Some had a happy outcome, but too many ended in heartbreak. So in moments like these, while she flew slowly over the ground, looking for survivors, she always tried to focus on those positive moments.

Holding the control stick of the Robinson R44 steady, she flew over the grid of coordinates that had been entered into her flight plan. It was a tedious task for sure, but the best way to conduct a thorough search.

Her aircraft had seating for four people: a single pilot and three passengers. Jason, the supervisory special agent, sat next to her. Two other FBI agents, one female and one male, sat in the back.

This mission was a bit of a cluster, and honestly, she wasn't sure what would happen if Decker Newcombe was found in the desert. But since all her passengers were FBI agents, she supposed that she wouldn't have to make any decisions about an apprehension.

In reality, they were searching for the nurse and the pilot. Farrah hadn't met Brett personally. Still, the piloting community in San Antonio was small, and she'd heard his name more than once. He had a reputation for being a solid person and a good pilot.

"Do you see anything out there?" she asked into her mic.

"Nothing yet." It was impossible to miss the frustration in Jason's tone.

Then again, they'd been flying for hours. She was tired and frustrated, too. If they didn't find someone—anyone—soon, they were going to have to turn back and get more fuel.

"What are the chances that this isn't where the cell phone is located at all and what we picked up was a mixed signal?" Jason asked. "Or that Newcombe took the phone and dumped it? He just wanted to send us on a goose chase."

Farrah wasn't sure if it was a rhetorical question or even if she should answer. Still, she knew a little bit about tech. "It's not like there are hundreds of towers for the phone to ping off of," she said. "But I can't guess about the man who's at large." She didn't even want to say his name. "You've studied him more than I have. What's your gut tell you?"

"The probability that the pilot and nurse survived the crash is pretty small. And even if they did survive, I'm not sure how far they'd make it with Decker on the loose," he admitted. "But while there's a chance they're out there, I'll do everything in my power to find them. How much longer can we stay in the air?"

She checked the fuel gauge. They didn't have a lot of gas in the tank, but it was enough to stay in the air a little while longer "The chopper can handle another pass before we'll have to refuel."

Staring out the windscreen, she softened her gaze. That was when she saw it, a wink of light coming from the ground. "Holy crap. Did you see that?"

Jason leaned forward in his seat until the webbing in his harness pulled tight. "See what?"

"There's something down there reflecting light." She turned the chopper's nose to the right. "On the top of that hill."

"There is?" Jason asked. "I don't see anything."

Had it all been in her mind? After all, she'd been flying for hours.

It came again. Just a wink, like the flash of a camera.

"You have to tell me you saw it that time," she said to the federal agent.

"I did. Is that them? I can't tell…"

Farrah pushed the throttle forward, and the Robinson shot through the sky. From a quarter of a mile out, she could see two figures standing on the top of the ridge and waving.

Using the chopper's radio, she placed a call to the sat phone.

"Marshal Reyes," said Farrah. "We have some people you need to come and pick up."

Chapter 16

Brett loved to fly. He liked helicopters more than he liked most people—his family notwithstanding. But he'd never felt as much joy as he did when the rescue helicopter banked to the right and started flying toward them.

Eva still wrapped her arms around his neck and leaned into him for support. He liked the feeling of her arms around his shoulders. Her body fitted perfectly next to his. How her breath washed over his ear. He wrapped an arm tighter around her waist.

"They do see us, right?" she asked.

The pilot of the aircraft dipped the aircraft from side to side. A pilot's way of saying hello. Waving with his free hand, Brett couldn't help but smile. "They see us all right."

The helicopter hovered over where they stood, the rotors sending a dust cloud rising from the ground. Eva tucked her head into his chest. He wrapped his arms around her, sheltering with his body. Nothing in the world had ever felt so right.

Shading his eyes from the dust, he studied the helicopter. Typically, Robinsons were rented by executives trying to avoid metropolitan traffic or tour companies taking sightseers over destinations, like the Grand Canyon.

But this one belonged to the Texas Rangers and was probably used for surveillance.

The pilot actuated the loudspeaker system. It was hard to hear her over the wind and the roar from the engine. But Brett could make out her words clearly enough.

"There's no place for me to land," she said. "A rescue party has been given your coordinates and will be to you within an hour. If anyone in your party needs medical attention, I can pull them up. But I'm low on fuel and don't have enough gas for much more airtime."

"You should go," Brett yelled in Eva's ear.

"I'm not leaving without you," she said. "We're a team, remember?"

He was tempted to let her stay with him. But her welfare was more important than what he wanted—which was to be with Eva.

"I'll be right behind you," he said. "Besides, you'll have to walk."

She shook her head. "I'm not going anywhere. Not when Decker is still out there. What if he comes back while we're gone and before the search party reaches you?"

"When Decker took the med kit, he got what he wanted. He's not coming back for me," Brett said, though he didn't exactly believe his own words.

"No way am I leaving you," she said.

The pilot was expecting some kind of response. He waved, a sure signal that they were okay.

The helicopter banked hard to the right and flew out

over the mountain. The downdraft washed over them, trapping them in a storm of dirt and grit.

Closing his eyes, he held tight to Eva. Soon, he'd have to let her go.

"You wait here," he said. "I'll go back to the cave and grab the food and whatever else was left behind. It won't take me long."

"Absolutely not." Eva fingers dug into his shoulder. "No way are you leaving me here alone. We're safer together."

How did she not understand that keeping her safe was the only thing that mattered to him? He'd survive and find help if only because it meant that he could send someone to help her. There was no way he could tell her that, not after she'd made it clear what she wanted—and didn't—from him. "But your foot," he began. Sure, it was an excuse, but it was also true. Eva had been injured.

"I'll be slow, but I'm coming with you."

"All right then." He wrapped his arm around her waist. "Don't be shy about leaning on me for support."

Slowly, they made their way back to the cave. The food and phones were just where they'd been left the night before. Eva dropped to the sandy floor.

"How do you feel?" Brett asked.

"Very relieved. It seems so strange to know that help is on the way. Soon, we'll be out of here and all of this will be over."

He knew how she felt. "I wasn't sure how we were going to survive this whole mess."

"I thought you were the optimistic one."

Honestly, he wasn't sure if she were teasing—or not.

But he didn't have the emotional depth to make jokes. Holding out his hand, he said, "I'll help you up."

She placed her palm in his. He pulled her to standing. For a moment, they just stood there, her hand in his. Her breasts pressed against his chest, and their hearts beat in sync. She lifted her eyes to his face. Their gazes met and held.

There was so much he wanted to tell her. That she was perfect for him in every way. That he admired her determination and strength even more than he admired her curves and beautiful blue eyes.

Now wasn't the time. Hell, maybe he never would find the right occasion. He squeezed her palm. "Can you stand?"

After letting her hand slip from his grasp, she said, "I can manage on my own."

For some reason, Brett knew she wasn't just talking about her injuries. He picked up the phones and the box of food. "We should probably head back to that ridge, just so the search-and-rescue team knows where to find us."

Eva just nodded and slowly walked out of the cave.

The sun had climbed in the sky. The air was warm, and the day promised to be dangerously hot. They took only a few steps when a male voice cut through the silence.

He couldn't make out the words, but he heard the tone and a pattern of speech. Was it Decker? Why would he come back if he had the medical kit? Then again, they had collected the rations. If the killer was going to survive, he needed food.

Until he knew who was out there, and what they wanted, they needed to stay quiet. The blood in Brett's veins turned to ice despite the heat. He stopped Eva with a hand on her arm.

She stood without moving. Obviously, she'd heard the voice as well, and they both shared a single question.

Was there any chance to face down the killer twice and survive?

Brett didn't have time to think about what to do next, when three people—a female and two males—crested the hill.

For a moment, nobody spoke. Then one of the men, who had a dark suntan said, "You must be Brett and Eva. I can't tell you how happy we are to have found you. I'm Ryan Steele. This is my boss at Texas Law, Isaac Patton. The lovely woman here is United States Marshal Maria Reyes."

"Stow the compliments, Ryan," said the marshal as she crossed the distance that separated them. "There will be plenty of time to debrief you both, but I figured you probably want these." She held out two plastic bottles filled with water. "I have a first aid kit as well. Looks like you both could use a little tending."

Without comment, Brett took the bottles of water. He handed one to Eva before unscrewing the cap of his own bottle. He drank, draining half the bottle in a single swallow. "How the hell did you find us?"

"That's a long story," said Ryan. "But we've got a bit of a hike ahead to get back to the command center, so there's plenty of time to tell it."

The marshal took over, bandaging the surface wound

on Brett's shoulder and giving both he and Eva some OTC pain meds. Eva was also given a set of collapsible hiking poles, which would help her to walk the miles back to their command post.

"Before we go," said the marshal as they prepared to leave, "I gotta ask about the prisoner. Did you see Decker Newcombe? Do you have any idea where he's gone?"

"We saw him all right," said Brett. "And as far as where he went, well, I couldn't really say."

She nodded. He could tell from the way she pressed her lips together until they lost their color that she wasn't satisfied with his answer. Still, the marshal knew she'd been told the truth. "Let's get going," she said.

And just like that, they were safe—or safer—and everything really had worked out.

Funny that in the moment, Brett was filled with regret. He should have told Eva how he felt about her. It seemed that he truly had lost his chance. Now, he doubted that he'd get another.

The hike back to the command center, which was actually at the initial crash site, was easier than Eva anticipated. There, another helicopter was waiting.

It took them directly to the hospital in Encantador. She'd been in the facility many times as a child and knew it well. There was an emergency clinic on the ground floor. On the second floor was a hospital with beds for two dozen patients. Most of them came from the clinic for acute care. Patients with any planned medical procedures traveled to a larger metropolitan area.

Eva and Brett had been sent to the emergency clinic.

They'd been placed in separate rooms in triage and were awaiting medical evaluation. Although to call it a room implied things that the space didn't have. It was more of a narrow cubicle, with room for a single hospital bed, a chair and not much more, with curtains for walls.

Eva had been given a set of scrubs to wear. The air cast removed, her leg was surrounded in ice packs and propped up on a pillow. She'd been given ibuprofen and hooked up to an IV of fluid to fight dehydration.

"How're you doing over there?" Brett's voice came from the opposite side of the thin cloth wall.

It was a loaded question, and she took a moment before answering. Overall, she was great—fabulous, really. Yesterday, she was certain she was going to die in the Texas desert—either of exposure to the elements or as another victim of a serial killer.

But while she'd rather be in the hospital than hiding in a cave, Eva wasn't completely pleased that they'd been saved. She just wasn't sure why.

Her grandmother—the whole reason she was part of the flight crew to begin with—was just one floor above her. It was torturous to be so close and still separated.

And she hadn't even begun to process the crash or the aftermath.

So...how was she doing?

"Physically, I'm okay," she said. "Emotionally..." Her words trailed off, not just because the fabric walls only gave the briefest nod to privacy but because, honestly, she wasn't sure how she felt.

"Knock, knock." The curtain between the two rooms fluttered for a moment before it parted, and Brett's face appeared. "I figured I'd come over and see how you're really doing. Want some company?"

"Sure." Her cheeks warmed. "How are you?"

Crossing into her room, Brett held on to the metal pole of an IV stand. A clear plastic bag hung from a loop. Tubing tethered him to the bag. "Hydration," he said, nodding toward the pole. "I feel fine, but the nurse insisted. They cleaned the wound on my shoulder. I was lucky, the bullet didn't hit the bone. The doctor put in a few stitches and told me to keep it covered for a few days. I have a prescription for an antibiotic. But I was lucky it wasn't worse, and no other serious injuries." He chuckled. "Guess I'll have a good story for the next pool party."

His face turned pale.

She realized his mistake the minute he spoke. There might be more pool parties in Brett's future. But none of them would include Wade. Or Lin. Or Stacy.

Her chest ached for him. She wanted to take his pain and make it her own. The thought left her breathless. When did she come to care so deeply and personally for Brett?

She thought she'd left his bed that morning because of Baba. But maybe she'd also come to fear the heartache that came after loving someone so completely that they became an extension of her soul. Not worrying about the joy but just fearful of the pain when they left.

Jeez, what a time to have an epiphany.

Then again, she supposed there was always going to be a clarity that came with facing death as many times as she had in the past forty-eight hours.

She couldn't say any of that, not now. Lines of sorrow were etched into Brett's forehead. So, she asked, "Do you want to talk?"

He worked his jaw back and forth. "Naw," he said, his voice hoarse. "I'm all right."

She doubted that was true. Still, she wouldn't press him to say anything he wasn't ready to talk about. "If you ever need anyone…"

"Yeah, yeah. I get it. Thanks." He dropped into a chair next to her bed. "How's the leg?"

It was fine with her if he wanted to focus on something that was less consequential that the death of his entire crew. She said, "Right now, it's cold and numb—which is a good thing."

Together, they'd survived a helicopter crash, being lost in the desert for the past day and an assault by a serial killer. Yet now, there was nothing for them to talk about other than the mundane.

Since she didn't have anything better to say, she added, "They're going to do an X-ray to make sure nothing's broken. Assuming it's not, then I'll have to see how it heals. Not a lot can be done for a sprain. But if I pulled or tore ligaments, I might need surgery. I'll get an MRI soon to check for head injuries. Any more sophisticated scans will have to wait until I'm at a larger medical facility."

He nodded. "And how are you?" he asked, his voice low. "Really?"

"It all seems surreal," she said. "I'm sure that eventually everything we've been through will hit me. But for now, the last twenty-four hours feels like a dream.

Or maybe this is the dream, and we're still out in the desert somewhere."

He scooted the chair closer, the legs scraping across the floor like nails on a chalkboard. He reached for her hand. "Are you going to be okay?"

"I'm not sure what being okay means anymore." She lifted the corners of her mouth, even though she didn't feel like smiling. "But I'll be all right." After all, she didn't have any other choice. Ready to change the topic, she asked again, "How are you?"

"Me? I'm fine. I don't even think I'm all that dehydrated."

"And emotionally?" she coaxed.

"I haven't even had time to think since the crash—only do what needed to be done to survive." His voice was hoarse, caught on emotion. He coughed. "I don't know what to do next, you know. Once we get out of here, I'll go back to San Antonio. But I'm not sure how I'm supposed to go back to work. I can't just get back in the air with a different crew—not right now, at least."

"What will you do?" she asked.

"Honestly, I don't know." He exhaled. "How about you?"

Her heart ached for Brett. They'd lived through the same harrowing day, but for him it was worse. He'd lost his coworkers and friends.

But she knew exactly what she was going to do next. "As soon as I get out of this bed," she said, "I'm going to go up to the second floor to see my grandmother. After I give her a big hug, I'll probably stay in town for a few days. I can stay with my sister and her family."

"Sounds nice," said Brett.

"I don't know that I'll get a lot of rest. Besides Katya and Jorje, I have two nephews and a niece. They're all adorable, but the kids have a lot of energy."

"I know how it goes. My sister has twin daughters. They're cute and all, but after a few hours of playtime—especially when I'm giving nonstop horsey rides—Uncle Brett needs a nap."

She smiled. "I bet you're a good uncle."

"I try." He gave her hand a squeeze. "Speaking of naps, I should let you rest. Drop me a line now and then."

She was reluctant to let him go and tightened her grip on his fingers. "Thanks for everything, Brett. I wouldn't have survived without you."

He opened his mouth, ready to say something. Then he shook his head, seeming to change his mind. "You take care of yourself."

Before Eva could say anything, the curtain next to the hall parted. It was US Marshal Marcia Reyes. "Hey, I hope I'm not interrupting anything."

Eva let go of Brett's hand. "Of course not," she said.

Maria stepped into the small cubicle, and three men followed. Eva recognized the duo from Texas Law—Ryan and Isaac—at once. The third man was tall with close-cropped blond hair. "We need to chat with you both about what happened out there." Maria nodded toward the blond man. "This is Jason Jones. He's with the FBI." She paused a beat. "He's got some questions."

Just like that first drop of a roller coaster, Eva's stomach plummeted and left her with a sick feeling. Were the authorities going to claim that somehow, as the two survivors of the crash, she and Brett were responsible? The chaotic moments right before the chopper went down flashed through her mind. It was all a jumble. Had she made a mistake? "The FBI? We didn't do anything wrong."

"I'm not accusing you of anything," said Jason. "But you understand that when a helicopter crashes, there's an inquiry. And when a serial killer gets loose, there's a full investigation."

His words did little to provide any comfort. "Okay."

Jason continued, "I also hate to tell you that this might drag on for weeks or even months. But for now, what I need is anything you might know about Decker Newcombe."

"What kind of things do you want to know?" Brett asked.

"Honestly, anything at all. What kind of interaction did you have with Decker? We assume he took Marshal Herrera's gun and his cash. Is he still armed? Do you have any idea where he might go?"

Brett spent a few minutes outlining the storm and the debacle in the back of the helicopter. He ended with the standoff this morning that ended with Decker armed and on the run and Eva being thrown over the side of a cliff. She added details when needed.

"I'm not surprised he pitched you into a ravine," said Isaac. "That's part of Decker's MO to escape. He threw my girlfriend out of a car just so I'd quit chasing him."

Ryan lifted his hand. "Same. He stabbed mine to distract her from continuing her investigation into his crimes. She still has nightmares."

Great. So not only did she have a long investigation to look forward to, but PTSD, as well. "It's good to know I'm not alone."

Isaac said, "I could arrange for you to talk to either Clare or Kathryn, if you want."

It would be a strange sisterhood—those who had survived Decker Newcombe. Still, "It might be helpful to talk to them," Eva said.

Isaac nodded. "I'll get you their numbers."

"Back to Decker," said Jason. "Is there anything important that you remember?"

Eva began to shake her head but stopped. "He wanted the med kit."

"Med kit?" Marcia repeated. "Was he injured?"

"In a way," said Eva. "He was having withdrawals from pain meds."

"And did the kit have the type of medications he wanted?"

Brett said, "We don't carry any controlled substances on the aircraft."

"I did tell him about naloxone."

They all stared at her.

"It helps with the physical symptoms of withdrawals," she said. "It's especially beneficial with opiates."

"That doesn't make sense." Ryan rubbed the back of his neck. "Decker never used drugs before."

"He blamed the hospital." Eva tried to remember everything he said. "He told me that he was addicted to 'the crap—'" she hooked air quotes around the words "—that the nurse had given him. He was never my patient, but I heard some news that mentioned his injuries when he was captured. All his wounds sounded severe. The protocol would be to give him something for the pain. There was probably a plan in place to ween him from his current dosage, but the helicopter crash derailed that treatment."

Ryan shrugged. "I guess it's no surprise that he's having issues, then."

"It's not," Eva agreed.

"Let's get back to the time you spent with Decker," said Jason. "Did he mention anything about where he might go or what he might do next? Even if it doesn't seem important to you, it could be a clue."

Eva drew in a single breath and exhaled slowly. Before, her memories had been a jumble. Now she had space to think. Still, nothing came to mind. She shook her head. "Sorry, I can't think of anything."

Jason held out a white business card with the FBI's seal. "If anything comes to mind," he said, setting it on the end of her bed, "reach out."

The curtains parted again. A female aide pushed a wheelchair into the cubicle. She had a small diamond stud in her nose, and the tips of her white-blond hair had been dyed pink. An ID lanyard around her neck read Andrea Carlson, Certified Nurse's Aide.

"Wow," said Andrea. "It's really crowded in here. But doctor's orders, the patient has to go for an X-ray. So you all will have to excuse me," she said before backing out and making room for everyone to leave.

"I'd appreciate it if you didn't speak to anyone about your encounter with Decker," said Jason. "Not now, at least."

"Is that an order?" Eva asked, bristling.

"More like a friendly request," he said.

Then, the quartet of law enforcement filed out of the room, leaving only Eva and Brett.

He pressed his lips to the top of her head. "You take care of yourself," he repeated.

Before Eva could say anything, Andrea returned with the wheelchair. "We're ready for your scans. First the X-ray and then the MRI." The other woman continued. "Of course you know all of this, but we don't have a lot of the fancy equipment you do at San Antonio Medical Center. Depending on what's wrong with your ankle, you might be transported to a larger hospital."

She recognized that the small hospital in Encantador didn't have the funding or the patient population that a medical behemoth like SAMC did. But she wasn't about to be taken out of the area until she saw her grandmother—a request she was certain Andrea would grant.

But Brett was another matter altogether.

Eva swung her legs over the side of the bed. Andrea held on to her elbow and guided Eva into the wheelchair. She turned her gaze to where Brett stood.

He parted the curtains between their cubicles and lifted his hand, giving her a wave. Then, he slipped between the seams and was gone.

Her eyes burned and her throat was tight. After everything she'd endured it'd be foolish to cry now. Two days ago she hadn't even known Brett. But she wouldn't have survived without him. That meant he was more than a temporary lover. He was also the man who saved her life.

Eva didn't know if he'd still be in the hospital by the time she was finished with her scans. Was this their final farewell?

Chapter 17

It didn't take long to get an X-ray of Eva's leg and an MRI of her skull. Back in the radiology department, Andrea was waiting with the wheelchair. As Eva eased back into the chair, she said, "My grandmother, Gladys Tamke, is a patient at this hospital. Is there any way I can see her?"

Andrea started pushing the wheelchair down a long hallway. "Because of the feds, the doctor gave strict orders that you can't have visitors until you're released. It really shouldn't be much longer. Once the scans are read, you'll be free to go."

She brought Eva back to the same triage room she'd occupied earlier. "Do you know if Brett is still here?" Eva asked.

"I think so." Andrea helped her back into the bed. "Do you want me to check?"

"Since the walls are cloth," said Brett, "I can hear you."

The curtain parted, and he appeared. He was no longer tethered to a pole with a bag of fluids.

"What happened to your IV?" Eva asked.

"They told me I'm free to go once I get the discharge papers," he said. "What about you? Is your foot broken?"

"Don't know yet."

"I'll check on those orders for you." Andrea slipped a pillow under Eva's foot. "Be right back."

Finally, they were alone. "I'm glad that you're still here," Eva said. "It was so rushed before that I didn't get to say goodbye properly."

"Obviously," he said, "I won't forget you."

She laughed. "Yeah, I guess not. How are you getting back to San Antonio?"

"I really haven't figured that out yet. I'm hoping I can catch a ride with someone, or the hospital will send somebody to get me. Once I get my phone, I'll call my folks in Dallas. I'm sure they'd come and get me, but it'd take them the rest of the day just to get here." He exhaled. "Maybe it's best if I just rent a car." He glanced in her direction. Eva's pulse quickened, just like always. "You can rent a car in Encantador, right?"

"I think there's a place about a mile out of town that rents cars," she said. Or maybe they only rented moving vans. "I've never had to do that here, so I don't know."

The curtains parted again, and a tall man with a sparse mustache entered the room. "Hi, I'm Dr. Flores. I looked over your X-rays and didn't see any broken bones. There might be other damage, like torn ligaments, so I'd like for you to check in with an orthopedist and also get a full-body MRI when you get back to San Antonio. Until you get to see a doctor, I'm going to refit you with another air cast for support. But I want you stay off that foot as much as possible. Other than that, all your labs look fine, and you're free to go." He held out a stack of papers in each hand, one for Eva and the other for Brett. "Both of you are free to go," he corrected himself.

With perfect timing, Andrea returned with an air cast.

Once the cast was in place, Eva swung her legs to the side of the bed and lowered herself slowly to the ground.

"How's that feel?" Brett asked, his hand under her elbow.

"Not bad."

Andrea removed Eva's IV. "Looks like you're all set. If you want to go to the second floor and check in with your family, I think there are a lot of people who'd like to see you."

Eva's chest filled with love for her family. "Thanks a million."

With a single wave, Andrea left the room. And once again, Eva was alone with Brett.

"Well, I guess this time," he said, "it really will be goodbye."

"I guess so." Her heart clenched. After such a short time, he'd become a mainstay in her life. What was more, she didn't want him to go. She reached for his arm. She wasn't ready for goodbye. Her fingers touched his wrist, and the fluttering in her middle returned. A flush crept up from her chest to her cheeks. When was the last time she'd had this kind of reaction to a man? Well, at least she knew that answer to that question. Brett really was one of a kind. "You take care of yourself. Send me a text now and then and let me know how you're doing."

"You aren't even going back to San Antonio? What about your job or your apartment?"

"My San Antonio apartment is a furnished rental, and the lease is almost up anyway," she said. Hell, the dishes weren't even hers. "All I need to pack up are my belongings, that won't take long. The job?" That was a little more complicated—although she didn't plan to be employed by SAMC by the end of the month. "After everything that happened over the past twenty-four hours, well, I need some time off."

"Maybe that's what I should do, too." He let out a long and loud exhale, a sure sign he was making a plan. Funny how after just a few days, she'd learned how to read Brett. In a lot of ways, she knew him better than almost anyone else—aside from her family, that is. "I might start looking for a new job. Maybe even relocate." He shook his head. "I don't know how I'm supposed to work at San Antonio Med without my crew. The ghosts of Wade and Stacey and Lin will always be in the flight facility." He held up a hand. "Like, I don't mean that they'll actually be haunting the place. It's just that I won't ever be able to walk through the door and not miss them like hell."

He studied the floor, as if the answers to the universe were written on the tiles.

She couldn't leave him alone, not when he was so glum. At the same time, the pull to be with her family was like iron to a magnet. "Before you go," she said, "would you like to meet my grandmother? She's upstairs. The nurse said my whole family is waiting."

"Your whole family?" He shook his head. "Oh no. I can't. I mean, I'd love to meet them all, but they're here for you."

"If it wasn't for *you*, I wouldn't be here for them to see." She gave his hand a squeeze. "C'mon, I'm sure they'll want to meet the man who helped get me here alive."

He shook his head again. For a moment, she was sure that he would refuse once and for all. Her chest ached. She knew it was best to ignore the feeling and whatever else it might imply.

"All right," he said at last. "I'd love to meet your family."

The flight suit, her shattered phone and her one remaining shoe had been stowed in a plastic bag with a drawstring closure. She picked up the bag and looped the string around her wrist. Brett picked up a similar bag from the foot of his bed.

"Baba's room is on the second floor," Eva said, exiting the triage cubicle.

"Baba? That's a cute nickname." Brett followed her into the corridor. On either side were curtained rooms.

This hospital was nothing like San Antonio Medical Center, with its top-notch treatment centers, state-of-the art equipment and world-class medical professionals. Would she really be able to leave all the hustle and bustle of a major hospital behind to work in a rural setting? She ignored the twisting in her gut.

"Baba is Ukrainian for grandmother."

"I like how it respects your heritage."

"If you like that," she said as they walked down the hallway, "then you'll love pierogis."

"Oh, I already love pierogis," he said. They'd reached the elevator. Stopping in front of the doors, he pushed the call button. "I know a place in San Antonio that serves the best pierogis."

"Until you've had my grandmother's pierogis, you haven't had pierogi. Trust me."

The elevator doors slid open, and they stepped inside. "I do trust you," he said with a smile.

She pressed the button for the second floor, and the elevator rose slowly. They stood side by side, his arm brushing her shoulder. Her skin warmed with the contact.

She wanted him to touch her more. To kiss her. To hold her. To beg her to come back to San Antonio and stay with him forever.

Then again, if he did, what would she say? Or do?

No, it was better that they part ways soon. She shouldn't have invited him to meet her family, but there was no turning him away now.

A *ding* sounded as the elevator staggered to a stop. The doors slid open, and without a word, Eva stepped into the hallway.

The scent of antiseptic and coffee and the sweetly rotting stench of illness hung in the air. It was the same olfactory miasma that permeated the corridors of San Antonio Medical Center. Hallways went off in four directions with a circular desk at the intersection, just like the nurse's station in SAMC's emergency department.

Then again, nursing was the same all over the world. There were people who needed care. It was a nurse's job to provide it. All the rest was just window dressing. Maybe she'd be okay working in Encantador, after all.

"They'll know my grandmother's room number," she said, inclining her head to the nurse's station.

A male nurse with dark hair and a name tag that read Dennis Wang looked up as they approached. "May I help you?"

"I'm Eva Tamke," she said. "My grandmother, Gladys Tamke, is on this floor."

From personal experience, she knew that gossip traveled fast in a hospital. That meant that Dennis was familiar with what had happened to both Brett and Eva. But he was a true professional and didn't mention anything about the ordeal. He glanced down at a clipboard. "Looks like your grandmother is West-11." He pointed down a hallway. "Second door from the end on the left."

She thanked him before turning down the corridor. Her boot clunked against the tile floor, matching the pulse that thundered in her ears. Soon, she was deaf to everything other than a single word she repeated over and over in her mind. *Family. Family. Family.*

The door didn't quite meet the jamb and sounds leaked out into the corridor. At once, she recognized her sister's alto voice and her laugh that was like music. Baba's voice was deep and gravelly—a side effect from age and a smoking habit she'd dropped decades earlier. There were giggles of children—so her nieces and nephews were at the hospital, as well.

She knocked, and the door swung open. The first person she saw was Katya, sitting with her back to the door. A toddler, her niece Abby, was cuddled on her shoulder. Abby looked up, smiling brightly, and squealed.

Katya turned in her seat and saw Eva. Jumping up,

she ran across the small room. The sisters embraced like that hadn't spoken in years—not just days.

Eva's eyes stung, and her throat was tight. "It's good to see you."

Tears ran down Katya's cheeks. "We've been waiting for news. But the hospital takes patient privacy very seriously." She hugged Eva tighter. "I can't tell you how worried we've been."

Eva kissed her niece on the cheek as Jorje approached. "Hey, I'm glad to see you up and about."

She gave her brother-in-law a quick hug. Then, she hugged each of her nephews.

Finally, on the bed near the window, was her grandmother. When had she gotten so frail-looking?

"Hey, Baba," she said.

Her grandmother opened her arms. Like she was a little girl with a skinned knee or a broken heart, Eva ran to Baba.

"I was worried I'd never see you again," the older woman whispered. "What in the world were you doing on a helicopter in the first place? I thought you gave all of that up when you left the national guard."

It was Eva's turn to cry. She wiped her eyes with the back of her hand. "I was on the flight because it was coming here."

It seemed like a million years ago when she and Brett had been in the flight facility at San Antonio Medical Center. She turned toward the door. Brett still stood on the threshold.

"There's someone I'd like you to meet." Eva held out her hand, and he came to stand with her. "This is

Brett Wilson, the medevac pilot. Without him, I never would've survived."

Brett gave her hand a squeeze. "I think she's giving me too much credit. Your granddaughter is an amazing woman. She would've done just fine without me."

Jorje held out his hand for Brett to shake. "It's nice to meet you. And thanks for taking care of Eva."

"She took care of me," Brett said as the two men shook hands.

"Sounds like you make a nice team," said Katya. "You were both fortunate to have each other."

Baba pushed a button on the side of her bed that lifted her to sitting. "Tell me—what happened? How did the helicopter go down?"

For a moment, Eva's memories dragged her to the helicopter's hold. Before the turbulence started, Decker lay in the bed, confused and in pain. He'd been mouthing words, most of which she couldn't hear.

But there was one thing she remembered.

Ana.

"I have to make a call," she said. "Does someone have a phone?"

Her sister held out a cell. "You can use mine."

She gave Katya's hand a squeeze as she took the device. Patting down the scrubs she wore, she checked for the business card that the FBI agent had placed on the end of her bed. She hadn't picked it up after all.

She wanted to curse.

"What's wrong?" Jorje asked.

"There's someone I need to call, but I can't find his business card."

"Who?" her brother-in-law asked.

"Jason." What was his last name? She turned to Brett. "You know, the FBI guy."

Slipping his hand into a pocket, Brett pulled out a small white rectangle of paper. "I got it right here." He held it out to her. "Why do you need it?"

"I just remembered something." Her heart was racing. "It might not be important, but it's not up to me to decide."

"You're calling an FBI agent?" Katya said. "What's going on?"

Eva hated to keep secrets from her family. But Jason had been clear—she shouldn't discuss Decker or his escape with anyone. "I'll tell you when I can." She needed privacy. Pressing the phone between both of her palms as if saying a prayer, she asked, "Can I bring this back to you in a minute?"

"Go," said Katya. "Make your call. We'll chat when you get back."

Eva stepped into the corridor, Brett right behind her. Every room was full. Nurses, aides and doctors roamed up and down the hallway. A janitor, pushing a bucket on wheels by a mop handle, walked past.

Brett placed his hand on her elbow, steering her toward a stairwell. "Let's try outside."

Their footfalls clanged on each step. The stairs ended at a heavy metal door that led outside. Brett pushed the door open and stepped onto a concrete pad. The South Texas sun beat down, shimmering in waves off the adjacent parking lot.

Cupping her hand over the phone screen so she could see, she entered the number for Jason's cellphone.

He answered after the second ring. "Agent Jones."

"This is Eva Tamke. You said to call if I remembered anything, and, well, I did remember something. I don't know if it's important or not."

"Eva, I'm with both Isaac Patton and Ryan Steele, and I've got you on speakerphone. Tell me what you remember. We'll figure out what it means on our end."

She glanced up at Brett. He gave her a nod of encouragement. "While we were flying, Decker was either in a state or talking in his sleep." She gave herself a moment to recall exactly what he'd said. "He asked, 'Ana, why did you go?' and also, 'Was it because of him?' I didn't know what he was talking about, but still you said to call."

"Ana?" Jason echoed. "That name doesn't ring a bell."

"Well, it does to me." She recognized Ryan's voice. "Years ago—God, it has to be more than a decade by now—he dated a woman named Anastasia Pierce. She just up and left him one day. Gave him a note that said something like, I can't do this anymore."

"We need to find out where Anastasia Pierce is now," said Isaac. "That way she'll know he's escaped, and even worse, he's thinking about her. Even if he was in a stupor, he might be thinking about going after her."

"Best I can recall," said Ryan, "is she was a grad student. She was studying biology or ecology or some such. She also worked at a coffee place part-time." He pulled a phone from his pocket and tapped on the screen. After a moment, he said, "That's weird."

The FBI agent drew his dark brows together. "What's weird?"

"She doesn't show up on a quick internet search," said Ryan, holding up his phone. Eva couldn't make out what was on the screen. "I mean, there's stuff about her. But old—there's an article she's mentioned in when she was in school. That's back when I knew her."

"That is strange," said Isaac. "Do you have any thoughts? You know her."

"Me?" asked Ryan. "I *used* to know Ana, but like I said, that was years ago. Maybe she's not real big on social media now that she's older."

"Or maybe she doesn't want to be found," said Isaac.

"Even if she isn't on social media," said Jason, "there are ways to find her."

Eva knew that eventually they'd find the woman— Anastasia Pierce. After all, one of them was with the FBI. The other two worked for some kind of private security firm. Still, she felt as if she were eavesdropping on their conversation. Besides, she wanted to get back to her family. "Well," she said, interrupting their brainstorming, "I hope that helps."

"It helps," said Jason. "If you remember anything else, let us know. Tell Brett to do the same."

She looked up from the phone and met his gaze. "I will."

The call ended, and she tucked the phone into the side pocket of her borrowed scrubs. She held out Jason's business card to Brett. "This is yours."

He waved it away. "You keep it. I didn't interact with Decker much, so there's not as much for me to remember."

He might be right. Still she said, "I have his number on my sister's phone. I can transfer it once I get a new phone for myself."

He took the card and shoved it into the front pocket of his pants. For a moment, they stood in the oven-like heat. Neither spoke.

Finally, Brett said, "Well, I guess I better get going. Your family seems really nice. Tell them I enjoyed meeting them all."

"You're welcome to come back to the room." She wasn't ready to part ways and never see him again.

"I appreciate your offer," he said, his expression unreadable, "but I have to figure out how I'm getting home. Besides, your family wants to see you—not entertain some random stranger."

Brett was much more than a random guy. Still, she had no other choice.

Now, it really was goodbye.

Chapter 18

Brett found a bench in front of the hospital and placed a call to his parents in Dallas. His mother wept when she heard his voice—the crash had made the news. His father, always stoic, said that he never doubted Brett's ability to survive. They promised to pass on the news to his sister, and he promised to come for a visit to Dallas soon. He knew his mother would be on the phone with Shannon as soon as they hung up.

But he didn't have any immediate plans to visit his family.

Looking over his shoulder at the hospital, he tried to figure out which window belonged to Eva's grandmother.

Brett's family had never been very emotive. He wondered what it would be like to have a boisterous and loving family like Eva's. Then again, he had other things to worry about beyond Eva and her kin. He had to get back to San Antonio, and honestly, he didn't know how he was going to make that happen.

Using his cell phone, he placed a call to Darla at SAMC's human resources.

The phone rang once. "This is Darla."

"Hey," he said, suddenly exhausted by the past twenty-four hours. "It's me. Brett."

"Omigod, Brett," she cried. "We've been worried sick about you and Eva. An FBI agent told us you'd been found and were being transported to the hospital in Encantador. How are you both?"

"Eva hurt her leg during the crash. She got an X-ray. Thankfully, nothing's broken. They don't have an MRI machine here, so she'll have to have more testing later. Other than that, she's okay."

"And how are you?"

"Me? I'm fine, physically, at least." Then again, he and Eva were the only two crew members to survive the crash. For the first time since going down, he thought of each of his friends in turn. Stacy, who was always serious. There was Wade, who loved to joke. Lin was forever cautious and careful. In fact, he'd warned against the flight. What would've happened if Brett had listened in the first place?

Suddenly, the sun became too bright. He closed them against the glare as tears leaked down the side of his face. He wiped his cheek with his shoulder.

"I'm so glad you're okay," Darla was saying. "We'd been told that there were fatalities. The feds are very hush-hush about what happened," she whispered. "But at least you're okay."

He wasn't sure if he'd describe himself as being okay. Still, he said, "I'm as good as can be expected." Exhaling, he started again, "I was calling because I'm not sure what happens next. I'll have to talk to the FAA and soon. Obviously, I can't fly my helicopter back to San Antonio, but I'm also not sure how to get back home."

Home. The word struck him in the chest. Would San Antonio ever feel like home again?

Darla said, "You let me worry about getting you back here. It might take some time. I'll reach out as soon as I have a plan," she said before ending the call.

He rose from the bench and walked toward the front doors of the hospital. They opened with a *swish.* After being in the sun and the heat, the inside was cool and dark.

A sign indicated that the cafeteria was to the left. His stomach grumbled and clenched painfully. It had been more than twenty-four hours since he'd eaten a proper meal.

He followed a set of arrows, and soon, the scent of grease and fried meat hung in the air. The cafeteria reminded him of the lunchroom at his elementary school. A stack of trays sat at the end of a metal counter, along with a rack filled with cutlery. The food sat in warming pans behind a glass case. All the workers wore white aprons and hairnets or baseball caps.

He took a tray and a set of silverware, along with a stack of napkins.

"What can I get for you?" asked a man in a ball cap. The words Encantador Hospital Food Service had been screen printed on the front.

Brett scanned the selections. Mashed potatoes. Meat loaf. Sliced roast beef in gravy. Green beans swimming in a buttery sauce. Chicken parmesan and pasta with marinara. He smiled. All of it was comfort food—and exactly what he needed right now.

"I'll take the roast beef and gravy, potatoes and green beans."

"You want gravy on those potatoes?" the man asked, filling a plate.

"Is there any other way to eat mashed potatoes?"

The man laughed. "I guess not." He handed Brett his order. "Drinks are over there." He pointed to a soda machine, an iced tea dispenser and several coffee carafes lined up among stacks of paper cups, lids and straws. "You pay the cashier on your way out."

Brett filled a cup with ice and tea before setting a lemon wedge on top.

The cashier sat on a stool behind the register. "What've you got?" she said, punching keys on the register. "That'll be seven dollars and eighty-two cents."

"That's it?" he asked. He couldn't buy a medium latte in San Antonio for less than eight bucks.

"That's it."

Somehow, Brett had kept his wallet through the entire ordeal. He found a ten-dollar bill and dropped the change into a wire basket with a handwritten paper sign that said Feeling Tipsy?

She smiled wider. "You have a nice day."

Only a handful of tables were filled. At one table, a family of four looked up as Brett came close. It was hard to miss the expectant expression on their faces. He figured they were waiting for news about a loved one.

Next to the window, a woman wearing a flight suit sat alone. Was that the pilot who'd spotted them from the air? So many people had worked hard during the search and rescue. He'd probably never get to thank them all. But at least he could tell the pilot how much she was appreciated.

Carrying his tray, he approached the table. "Pardon me," he said. "Can I join you?"

With a smile, she scooted a Styrofoam cup closer to her empty plate. "Have a seat."

"I'm Brett Wilson, by the way." He sat down.

"Farrah Kaufman," she said. "Nice to meet you." She paused. "I'm glad to see that you're up and around, by the way."

"So, you are the pilot who spotted us?"

"Guilty as charged."

"I want to say thank-you, but that doesn't seem like enough. Can I get you a dessert or something?"

"Ugh." She pressed her hand to her stomach. "I've eaten too much already. My girlfriend is into competitive bodybuilding, we eat a lot of lean protein and steamed veggies. I thought food like this would be a treat. It was while I was eating. Now?" She pushed her plate away. "But you don't have to thank me. It's all part of the job, you know that."

"When you're the one on the ground hoping to be spotted by an aircraft, it feels pretty personal." He stirred the gravy into his potatoes and took a large bite. The potatoes had an earthy taste and a creamy texture. The gravy was savory and salty. Pointing to his food with his fork, he said, "Now that's good."

Farrah glanced over her shoulder before leaning forward. "Do you know anything?" she asked, "About Decker Newcombe, I mean."

As a fellow pilot, he felt he could talk to Farrah about the case. It was just that he didn't know much of anything. Brett shook his head. "Eva thinks he was suffering from withdrawals from all the pain meds he'd been given. It makes sense because he stole the medical kit and ran off."

"Any idea where he's headed?" she asked.

Brett took another bite and shook his head. "No idea." He didn't want to talk about the serial killer anymore. "So what's your story? How'd you become a pilot?"

"I flew in the navy for a few years. Got out and applied to work for the Texas Rangers. I was doing a sweep over the southern border when I got the call to come and look for you." She leaned back, stretching her shoulders over her chair. "In the past day, I've spent eleven hours in the air. I'm exhausted."

Regulations allowed for a pilot to spend only eight hours of flight time in a twenty-four-hour period. "Sounds like you've earned some time off."

"That I have," she said. "There's a little motel in town called the Saddle-Up Inn. I'm staying the night and then flying back to San Antonio in the morning. You're welcome to hitch a ride with me if you want."

Honestly, he wanted to get back before tomorrow. But he knew that waiting for Farrah might be his best option. "I'm supposed to hear back from the hospital soon. But if they can't get me back before tomorrow, I'll take a seat in your aircraft." He took a large bite of food.

"I'll be honest with you." Leaning forward, Farrah

used a conspiratorial tone. "I don't like the idea of staying in Encantador. Not with Decker Newcombe on the loose, at least. He's as bad as they come, and I've met some real scumbags in my life."

He agreed with her but said nothing. Giving a slight nod, he kept eating.

Farrah continued, "What do you want to bet that he's headed our way? He seems to have something against this town—this place—and I don't want to be here when he comes back filled with vengeance."

If he were being honest, Brett felt that her fear was overblown. He wiped his lips with a paper napkin. "I don't think he'll make it here. Or anywhere else for that matter."

"Why's that?" Farrah asked.

"First of all, the odds are against anyone surviving in the desert for long," he said. "The last time I saw Decker, he was sick. He didn't have any food or water. Hell, he wasn't even wearing a shirt—just a windbreaker he stole from a US marshal he killed."

"Yeah," she said, interrupting. "That's exactly what I'm talking about. Despite everything you said, he still killed a guy. Plus, it was a marshal who was armed and trained to use his weapon."

She had a point. Brett shrugged and took another bite. "I assume there are still aerial searches for Decker going on now?"

"You know how that goes. It's hard to spot anything from the air. If he doesn't want to be seen, he can hide—nobody'd be the wiser." Farrah was right about that, too. "Plus, it's too damn hot to use FLIR."

A forward-looking infrared sensor mounted to the nose of an aircraft could pick up heat signatures on the ground. Then again, there had to be a temperature differential for the equipment to be effective. And right now, it was, as Farrah said, too damn hot.

"They can use that at night," he reasoned.

"I hate the idea of spending the night here," Farrah repeated. "I just want to get home to my girl and put all of this behind me." She leaned back in her seat. "Not that I regret finding you and your nurse friend."

Suddenly, he wasn't hungry anymore. The food in the hospital cafeteria really was delicious and leaving a single bite somehow felt like quitting. Still, he pushed his plate away and said, "Too bad I'm not able to fly your chopper. That way we could both get out of here today."

"You know." She tapped a fingernail on the table. "That's a good idea. I'd have to get approval first, and it could take hours to get. But it'd be less time than the twenty-four hours I'm required to wait. Sit tight while I make a couple of calls."

"Where else am I going to go?" he asked, taking a sip of tea.

Farrah pulled her cell from the sleeve pocket of her flight suit. "I hope this works," she said, "because I can feel it in my gut. Decker's heading this way."

"You have a feeling in your gut?" Brett joked. "I thought that was all the hospital food."

"Well, there's that, too," she said with a laugh. "Hang on for a minute. I'll be back."

As she left, Brett looked around the room. The other

patrons had gone, and he was alone. In the silence, with nothing to do beyond listen to his own thoughts, he wondered about the missing killer.

Either Decker *was* hanging around—maybe to get rid of him and Eva for daring to thwart him—or he was on his way to wherever this Ana woman lived.

Neither was good.

Decker had gotten his craving for pain meds and the agony from withdrawals under control by taking a cocktail of naloxone and over-the-counter meds. Without the constant pain and nausea from before, he was able to think.

After killing a district attorney in Wyoming, Decker had lived off the grid around the border between the US and Mexico for over a year. He knew exactly where he was going.

It didn't take him long to find the dirt road and head south. He started to walk, every so often glancing over his shoulder. Too soon, he saw a cloud of dust billowing on the horizon. It was a vehicle heading his way.

If he was lucky, it was just someone using the little-known bypass. If it was someone with Homeland Security or people from another agency, well, then Decker's luck might've finally run out.

The gun hung from the back of his pants, hidden by the jacket. The cold metal dug into his spine. He had no problem shooting a cop. But by now whoever was on the road had spotted him and would notice if he reached for his weapon.

"Just play it cool," he said aloud.

As if answering, a hawk cried out as it circled overhead.

Dirt, caught in the breeze, wafted over him and he knew that the vehicle was close. He continued to walk. A moment later, he heard the sickly the cough of a motor. So, it wasn't law enforcement. If it was, the engine would be in tip-top shape.

His shoulders relaxed. His gait loosened. At times like this, he liked to think of himself as a lion on the Serengeti.

The cloud of dust surrounded him as an old truck rattled up to his side and stopped. The idling engine sounded like an old man with pneumonia.

He turned to the vehicle. A kid with dark hair and eyes leaned his elbow on the windowsill. Decker wasn't good at guessing the age of anyone—children especially. But he'd say the boy was either eight or nine years old. Behind the steering wheel was an old man with weathered skin and a straw cowboy hat. The man was a hundred years old if he was a day. Neither grandson nor grandfather were an immediate threat.

"You lost or something?" the kid asked.

"Since it's such a nice day, I'm just out for a walk."

The kid looked over his shoulder and translated for his grandfather. *"Como hace un día tan bonito, saldré a dar un paseo."*

The old man spit a long string of tobacco juice out the open driver's window. He grumbled, *"Idiota."*

Decker didn't need a translator to know what *that* meant.

The kid said, "My grandfather wants to know if you need a ride."

"Is that so?" he asked. "How far south are you going?"

"We'll cross the border, and then our ranch is another fifteen miles."

It wasn't as far as he needed to go. Yet he'd get there quicker by riding in the old truck than walking. It'd also keep him off the road and out of sight of any aircraft looking for him. Besides, he could always steal the truck later if he wanted.

"Much obliged," he said.

Decker opened the passenger door, and the kid slid to the middle of the bench seat. Settling in next to the boy, Decker pulled the door closed. The tires rolled forward, kicking up a rooster tail of dust.

The child studied Decker as the truck rumbled down the road.

After a moment, he glared at the boy. "What?"

"You a lawman?"

He choked out a laugh. "Me? Naw, kid. I'm no lawman."

"Why're you wearing that jacket, then?"

The child was clever, observant and maybe a little too shrewd for his own good. Decker was still wearing the marshal's windbreaker. "This?" He pulled on the collar. "It's a costume."

"It looks pretty legit to me."

Decker's temper flared. "Have you ever seen a real-life US marshal before?"

As if the kid had been scalded by Decker's anger, he scooted closer to his grandfather. "No."

"Besides, why would a US marshal be walking

through the desert without any goddamn shirt? Answer me that if you're so brainy."

"I don't figure one would," said the little boy.

"I don't figure one would, either." Decker pulled the windbreaker across his chest and looked out the window. The color brown stretched out as far as he could see. Umber earth. Sienna rocks. Even the trees were withered and covered with dust, the leaves were more tan than green. An angry sun hung in an azure sky. Both seemed intent on baking the earth until there was nothing left but coffee-colored dust.

He could feel the kid's gaze on him like a tickle on his cheek. He glanced over at the child. "What now?"

The boy regarded him with large brown eyes, so dark they almost looked black. "If you aren't a lawman, are you a bad man?"

From the other side of the cabin, the grandfather regarded Decker, as well. He had the same eyes as the kid—just decades older. It seemed like the old man understood English better than he'd originally let on.

Decker looked back at the little boy and placed his hand on top of his head. "Am I a bad man?" he repeated with a smile. "I'm the worst man you ever met, and you should stop asking questions."

The boy's eyes went wide. Like his head was on a swivel, he turned to his grandfather. The old man held on to the steering wheel with both hands. His knuckles were white.

"Just keep driving." He kept his tone pleasant. "And we can all part ways as friends." He wasn't sure if it was a lie or not. He really didn't like the idea of killing children—especially one who was so young.

But even a child could become a witness. And from here, Decker planned to vanish.

Chapter 19

The old man and the boy dropped Decker off at the end of a long, narrow track. It was as far as he wanted to go. He'd considered killing them and taking their truck. But in a way, the kid reminded him of the son he didn't know. As he walked down the dirt road, he wondered if he'd made a mistake in letting them live. Then again, he never did care much for killing children. And given the way he'd been torn from his own son, he didn't want to do the same to this kid.

The lane ended at a small house with cinderblock walls, a tin roof and a plywood door. A sagging sofa sat next to the door in a sliver of shade thrown off by the house itself.

Each step crunched with the gravel underfoot, so he wasn't surprised to see the old woman, Juanita, appear at the door as he approached. Her once-black hair was now gray. She wore it in a long braid that dangled over her shoulder like the tail of a hangman's noose. She had on a housedress and plastic flip-flops. Her upper arms were fleshy, and her feet were covered in grime.

Parked in front of the house was a white sedan. It was the same vehicle he'd purchased for her years earlier. But that was when he was working regular and was flush with cash.

"What are *you* doing here?" Juanita asked.

The year that Decker had lived off the grid, he'd stayed in a similar house only miles from here. He'd chosen the location because it was close to the old woman. During that time, he'd paid her well to bring him food, water and information.

He didn't trust her, per se. But that was because Decker didn't trust anybody, not really. Yet Juanita had proved to be useful. She was willing to do almost anything if it meant that she got some cash.

Before kidnapping the undersheriff's daughter, he'd left a box of belongings with the old woman. He'd also paid her two hundred dollars to keep it all safe.

In the box was an extra set of clothes and new shoes, but what he really needed was his cell phone. To find out the truth about his kid, he had to talk to Seraphim. That phone was the only way he had to make contact.

Their relationship was purely transactional. And yet, he gave her a slow smile. "Is that any way to greet an old pal like me?"

"We aren't pals," she said. "I heard you killed a lot of people. The federales came to my house. I was questioned and detained for days."

The fact that the Mexican police had traced him to Juanita's door came as a surprise—and not a pleasant one. "What did you say?"

"I didn't say nothing. But they kept me in a stinking cell for days. I still have nightmares."

Her suffering wasn't his problem. He shrugged. Then

he realized it *was*. If he didn't make her silence worth her while, she'd talk.

The woman continued, "I also heard you'd been taken to jail."

"Looks like I escaped." He sat on the old sofa. God, it felt good to sit down. He set the med kit on the ground next to him. "You got some water for me?"

"You got money?"

From the front pocket of his pants, he pulled out the cash he'd taken from the US marshal. He held up the folded bills before shoving them back in his pants pocket. "I got money."

She disappeared inside the house and returned with a plastic bottle of water. "For you."

He broke the seal and pulled the cap off. Then he lifted the bottle to his lips and drained it in a single swallow. The water hit his middle, and his gut cramped. Holding on to his side, he cursed. But the pain passed as quickly as it had come on. He held out the bottle to the old woman. "You got another one of these?"

She took the empty and folded her arms across her chest. "What do you want?"

"I need my stuff."

She held out her hand, palm up. "I need two hundred dollars."

His pulse spiked, and his heartbeat echoed at the base of his skull. "You what? I paid you when I dropped off the box."

"You paid me to keep the box," the woman said. "Not to give it back to you. I need money for that, too."

He pulled the cash out of his pocket and counted the

bills. "Fifty-seven dollars. That's all I got." He opened the windbreaker, showing his bare chest. "Hell, I don't even have a shirt on my back to give to you. But you can have all my cash. Take it or leave it."

"Leave it," she said, flipping the braid over her shoulder.

"You're kidding, right? After all I gave you, you can't just turn your back on me."

She lifted a single brow. "I can't?" With that, she turned and walked back into her house. She slammed the door shut. From where he stood, he could hear the click as she engaged the lock.

Decker typically wasn't a generous man. But he'd paid the old woman well for the care she provided along with her loyalty. Now, it seemed like his money had been wasted. He was beyond angry. He was furious. And if she thought something as flimsy as a door lock was going to keep him out, she was sorely mistaken.

He stood. Striding to the front door, he removed the gun from the back of his pants. He struck the wood with the butt end of the firearm. "Open the damn door."

"Go away," she said. "I've got a gun. If you come inside, I'll shoot you dead."

Yeah? Well, Decker had a gun, too. "I don't like to be threatened." His jaw was tight. "And if you don't open this door, I'm coming in anyway, and then, you'll be sorry."

"I don't like to be threatened, either," she said. "Leave, or I will call the federales. Then, they'll come and get you and stick you in a cell. You're the devil."

He'd been called worse, so her words didn't bother

him. But he'd done right by this woman for years. To have her betray him now was a blow he refused to ignore. He kicked the door handle. The lock held, but the wood splintered. He kicked it again, and the door swung open.

He doubted that she had a gun, but he wasn't going to risk getting shot. Dropping to one knee, he peered into the house. It was a single room with a bed in one corner, a small dresser at the end and a nightstand at the side. A round wooden table sat in the middle of the room, along with two mismatched chairs. A single bulb on a wire hung over the table. Against the far wall was a sink, a small stove and a refrigerator that was so old it could be considered an antique.

But the woman was gone.

Decker rose to his feet.

The door came at him, hitting him hard in the face.

For a moment, his eyes watered, and white dots floated in his vision.

The woman stepped out from behind the door. She held a rusty revolver that was as old as the fridge. She pointed the barrel at his chest. "I've shot men before," she said. "I might be old, but my aim is still good. Turn around and leave."

"I'm not going anywhere without my stuff." True, he didn't have money. But he did have medicine. Out here, where there were no luxuries and even necessities were hard to come by, the med kit might be worth something. "I got a medical kit from the air ambulance that was taking me to jail." He'd keep the remaining Naloxone for himself, but he didn't need the rest. "You can have it all.

Save it. Sell it. I don't care. Just give me my belongings, and I'll be gone."

"I don't care if you gave me a million dollars. Leave now and don't ever come back."

Honestly, Decker was done with the woman. She might have a gun, but she hadn't pulled the trigger. From his experience, it meant that she wasn't going to shoot. Also, she hadn't told him that his box of stuff was gone. He figured it was still in the small house, somewhere. All he had to do was go inside and get it for himself.

He crossed the threshold.

"I told you to leave," she said, pulling back on the hammer with a *click*.

For a single moment, Decker was eight years old. His mother's latest loser boyfriend had come home drunk and mean. There'd been a fight. They always fought. It was hard to ignore the yelling and cursing since Decker didn't have his own room in the drafty trailer. He slept on the sofa.

The loser boyfriend had shoved a gun in his mother's face. Then, he'd pulled back the hammer. *Click.*

At eight years old, there wasn't much Decker could do except cry. Yet, in that moment, he swore he'd never be the victim again.

Without thought, he lifted his gun and fired.

The bullet punched a hole through her housedress, and the old woman's eyes went wide. The faded fabric turned red as blood bloomed across her chest. She stumbled to the floor. The gun fell from her hand and skittered away.

Decker came forward and looked down at her. She

clutched her chest and gasped for breath. "You know," he said. "It didn't have to be this way."

"You are the devil," she said.

"Could be," he agreed. Although, he wasn't sure if she'd heard him. The woman was dead.

Juanita had shoved his belongings, as well as the box, under her bed. He changed his clothes and pulled out the phone. He pressed the power button. There was only ten percent battery left. But it was enough. He placed a call.

It was answered after the second ring.

"Yes?" The voice was electronically disguised. It reminded Decker how little he knew about Seraphim. Only communicating online, he'd never met the hacker in person. If they spoke via video, they wore a plague doctor mask and black leather gloves. The background was a black drape, and their voice was always altered to the same obnoxious squawk.

Decker didn't know the hacker's location, age, race or even their gender. Still, he said, "You know who this is."

"The last I heard you'd been captured and were going to jail."

"There was a change of plans," he said. And then, "I need all the information you have about Ana Pierce."

"There's not much about her on the internet. I've been looking for her and her son, but so far, I don't have much."

"He's my son, too." Or at least, that was what Decker intended to find out.

"I'll contact you if I need anything," he said, ready to end the call.

"Since you're free, what are your plans?"

"Me? I'm going to find my son. And you're going to help me." He found a slip of paper and a pen and wrote down Seraphim's phone number. Ripping off the sheet of paper, he shoved it into his pants pocket. Had Ana hooked up with a long string of loser boyfriends over the years? Was she married? Well, he was about to ruin whatever life she had—once the hacker found her, that is.

He took a few minutes to rummage through the old lady's kitchen. He found a case of bottled water, a box of cereal and a loaf of bread. It was enough food to get him where he needed to go. In a drawer of the small nightstand, he found the car keys.

Tucking everything in the box and picking up the med kit again, he left the house. Decker didn't bother closing the door. The sooner the wild reclaimed this house, the better.

As he drove down the narrow lane, he threw his old phone out the window. Decker was back, and nothing was going to stop him now.

It was 10:00 p.m. in London, England. Theo Fowler was still at his office on the fourth floor of the US embassy. He didn't mind being at work and not out at a pub like many of his coworkers. Hours earlier, he'd heard that the helicopter carrying Decker Newcombe had crashed in the Texas desert. Once again, the killer was at large.

He'd spent the last several weeks trying to unravel an online knot to find the elusive Seraphim, the hacker who'd helped Decker. So far, all he had to show for his efforts was a phone number that the hacker rarely used.

But if Decker had the chance, he might place a call to that number.

Theo's computer pinged, and an automated message bubble appeared. You have one message.

He reread the message several times. Someone had called the hacker, after all.

From the NSA's database, it only took a few moments to locate the origin of the call—several miles south of the US/Mexico border. Reaching for his own phone, Theo placed a call.

It was answered after the first ring. "Special Agent Jones."

Theo had only been given the barest of briefings on Decker Newcombe, but he had a gut feeling that Jason Jones, the supervisory special agent out of San Antonio, would once again be the FBI's point man on the case. "Jason, this is Theo Fowler. I have a hit on a cell phone used by Seraphim. I found where the call originated." He read off the coordinates. "It looks like the call came from Mexico, not far south of the border."

"That might be our man," said Jason. "You're a lifesaver. Tell the NSA to be careful. I might steal you away and put you to work for the FBI."

Theo sighed. When people said things like that, he didn't know how to react. Was it a compliment? A threat? "Well," he said after an awkward pause, "we'll see."

Over the years, he'd learned that a neutral response usually made everyone happy.

"Thanks again for the tip," said Jason. "I'll be in touch."

Theo ended the call and rose from his desk. He liked living in Britain, the British people and their culture. But lately he'd been thinking about home. Was it time for Theo to move back to the US?

If he did, he wouldn't want to work for the FBI. Maybe there was something else he could do?

Brett still hadn't heard from either Darla or Farrah. Without a solid plan, he was in limbo, waiting in the hospital cafeteria. He refilled his iced tea at the dispenser and took a sip.

The air in the room changed, and he knew that Eva was close. Or maybe it was just his imagination because he wanted to see her so damn bad. He looked up.

As if she'd stepped out of a dream, she stood on the threshold.

He wanted to smile. He needed to play it cool. After taking another sip of tea, he said, "Hey."

It took everything in him not to pull her to him, wrap his arms around her, feel her against him again. He'd missed her so much in the short time they'd been separated.

But she'd made her decision, and he had to respect that. Dammit.

"Hey, yourself," she said, and for a moment, there seemed to be something in her eyes. Like she was fighting her own feelings. Maybe that was wishful thinking, too. "I thought you were heading back to San Antonio."

"I was," he said. "I mean, I am. Or I will be, once a few things get straightened out. How's your grandmother?"

"Right now, she's sleeping. Katya and Jorje took the kids home."

"And you didn't go with them?"

Eva shook her head. "I'm going to stay here for a while, but I'm starving."

"I can vouch for the mashed potatoes." Then, he joked, "I mean, they aren't as good as my pancakes, but you know."

"I keep hearing that from you. Makes me think I missed out on something special."

He didn't know what to make of her comment. Was there more to her words, or was she just joking? He heard her place her order at the counter—"Hot roast beef, potatoes, gravy, green beans"—and he chuckled.

"What's so funny?" she asked, sitting back down with her food.

"That's exactly what I ordered."

"Oh yeah? Must be the meal of choice after being lost in the desert," she said. "Can you join me?"

Several pithy answers came to mind. He ignored them all and said, "I'd love to. What do you want to drink?"

"I'll take a caffeine-free soda."

Brett filled a paper cup with ice before filling it with ginger ale at the drink station. He set the cup next to her tray. "Here you go."

"Thanks." She reached for the cup and straw. "This all looks good."

"It's perfect comfort food," he said, sitting across from her.

After everything they'd been through together, it seemed like they should talk about something more than the quality of hospital food. Then again, maybe their relationship was over, and there was nothing more to say.

He waited as Eva ate her first few bites. Using her fork to point to her plate, she said, "This is really, really good."

"Agreed."

"I wonder what he wants." Still using her fork, she pointed to the door.

Brett turned to look.

Ryan Steele stood on the threshold and scanned the room until his gaze landed on Brett and Eva. He hustled across the floor to them. "Hey, man," Ryan said. "You know where Farrah went?"

"She's checking with her boss to see if they'll let me fly back to San Antonio."

"What do you mean," Ryan asked, "you're going to fly?"

He wasn't surprised that the security operative didn't know the FAA's rules. There was no reason. "A pilot can only be in the air eight out of every twenty-four hours. According to Farrah, she spent eleven hours in the cockpit and is grounded until tomorrow."

"But you can fly," Ryan clarified.

"I can."

Ryan narrowed his eyes. After a moment, he nodded his head, seeming to come to some sort of agreement with himself. "We've gotten some intel, and I need a pilot."

"What kind of intel?" Eva asked. She'd already eaten all the potatoes and gravy, along with half the roast beef. The green beans remained untouched.

"We think that Decker made a phone call about twenty-five miles from here. If I can get you authorized to fly that helicopter, could you take it up in the air?"

Brett was on his feet before he realized that he'd stood. "If you get me authorization," he said, "I can."

Ryan slapped him on the shoulder. "Meet you at the helipad in ten minutes."

"I'll be there."

He waited until Ryan had left the cafeteria before speaking. "It'll be good to get into the air," he said. But there was more. Eventually, Eva was going to walk out of his life. He didn't know how long it would take to apprehend Decker—that was if they even found him. And by the time Brett made it back to the hospital, she'd likely be gone. "Well, I know we keep saying this, but I guess this time it really is goodbye."

She stood.

He opened his arms. "I hope this time I can get a hug."

"You don't need a hug," she said. "This isn't goodbye."

"It's not?"

"It's not," she echoed. "Because I'm coming with you."

Chapter 20

Eva left the cafeteria and walked quickly to the nearest elevator. As the car rose slowly, she had to ask herself a single question.

What was she doing?

The last time she'd been in the air, the helicopter crashed. After a day of being stranded in the desert, she'd been rescued. For that, she was truly lucky. So many things could've gone differently, and she wouldn't have made it home.

If all of that was true, then why had she volunteered for the mission?

Decker had been her patient before. Certainly, he wasn't her responsibility now. Or was he?

The car jerked to a stop with a *ding*.

It was true that Eva didn't understand her own motivations. But she did know what she needed if she was going to get in the air again. It started with getting her flight suit. It was still in the hospital bag, which was still in her grandmother's hospital room.

After pushing open the door, she peered inside. Her grandmother lay on the bed, her eyes closed.

The bag leaned drunkenly against the leg of a chair—the same place she'd dropped it earlier. Without making a sound, she lifted the sack from the ground.

As she stood up straight, her grandmother's eyes were open.

"I didn't mean to wake you," Eva whispered.

"Oh, you didn't. It was Dennis. He's a nice man, but all day and all night, people are coming into the room. They want to take my blood pressure. My temperature. Look in my eyes with a blinding light. Who can sleep with a light like that shining in their eyes?" Baba gave a quiet chuckle. "You know, the doctor wanted me to stay in the hospital to get some rest. I've only taken cat naps since I got here. I'll need to go home just to get a full night's sleep."

It was a common enough complaint from patients. And Eva was happy that Baba had found some levity in a serious situation. Still, she didn't have much time to talk. "When I get back, we need to talk about plans for you."

"Oh no," Baba moaned. "Have you and Katya joined forces? Are you going to tell me that I need to move, too?"

"No, Baba. It's not that at all." She really didn't have time for this conversation and silently cursed that she'd brought up the subject in the first place. But she had, and there was no sense leaving her elderly grandmother with more worry. "I was thinking I could come here and live with you."

"What about your job? Your friends? Your apartment?"

They were all things that Eva had considered. Much as she'd told Brett, she said, "I can get out of the lease to my apartment with a month's notice. Obviously, I'd work here. And my friends in San Antonio will still be my friends. But you are family. You are who's important."

"I can't let you do that," said Baba. "You have a life already. Besides, you don't want to take care of an old lady."

Eva could feel the seconds slipping away with every beat of her heart. Reaching for her grandmother, Eva gave her hand a squeeze. "We can talk more when I get back. But right now, I have to scoot."

Baba tightened her grip, refusing to let go. "Where are you going?"

The FBI agent had warned against talking to anyone about Decker being on the loose. Then again, Baba wasn't just anyone. "I was on the medevac because we were transporting a patient." Glancing over her shoulder, she made sure nobody was standing next to the door. As far as she could tell, they were alone. Still, she lowered her voice. "The patient survived and is still out there. But the patient is…" she paused, trying to find the right word to describe the serial killer "…important."

"You had someone important on the air ambulance? Who?"

She really should follow the agent's orders, yet she found herself saying, "It was him, Baba. Decker Newcombe."

Baba sucked in a single breath, and her complexion paled. "He's back? Are you joking?"

"Honestly, I don't know much. The authorities think he made a phone call."

"But why you?" her grandmother asked, echoing Eva's own questions.

It was then that she understood her own mind and heart and soul. She was doing this all for Brett. It was more than the fact that they'd made love—in his home. In the cave. The two of them really had become a team. So, if he was going after Decker, she was, too.

How was she supposed to say any of that to her grandmother?

Baba's fingers dug into the back of Eva's hand. "I don't like that you'll be involved in looking for that fiend. But you're a strong, smart woman, an excellent nurse, and that gives me comfort. You do what you need to, but be careful. When you get back, we'll talk more."

Eva placed her lips on her grandmother's forehead. Her skin was thin and dry. Nobody knew what the next year or month or even day would hold. But for now, she knew what she needed to do Yet, her pulse raced. Was she really about to face down the killer again?

For an instant, Eva was a little girl, coming to her grandmother for comfort and support. The thought of remaining with Baba came and went. But if Brett was going out again, so was she.

Walking across the room, Eva paused at the door. Baba lifted her hand, giving a final wave. Then the older woman settled into her pillow and closed her eyes.

Eva stepped into the corridor and retraced her steps to the elevator.

Dennis looked up as she passed the nurse's station. "How's your grandmother?" he asked.

"Good," said Eva. "She's resting now."

"I'll let her get some sleep before checking on her vitals again," he said. "Can I help you with anything else?"

She shook her head, ready to say no. Then again… "Do you have a well-stocked first aid kit I can take with me?" If she was going with Brett again, she should at least make herself useful. That meant being prepared.

"I can get you something," he said. "I probably shouldn't ask what's going on, should I?"

"The less I have to say, the better."

"Got it." Dennis moved out from behind the counter. "Be right back."

He returned a moment later with a medical kit much like the one she'd had on the medevac out of SAMC. Thanking him, she left the hospital.

The heliport was just a square of concrete with a pump for fueling aircraft. Next to the helipad was a small hangar with two rooms—a lounge with a sofa, chairs and a TV on a stand, and a gender-neutral restroom. The hospital in Encantador didn't have the funds to pay for its own aircraft or a crew. But being so far away from any major cities, often a medevac was the only way to get patients to larger facilities.

Quickly, Eva changed into her flight suit in the bathroom. Brett hadn't been given clearance to pilot the aircraft, yet he'd changed, as well. They waited next to a helicopter that sat on the helipad.

Four people approached—Ryan, Isaac, Jason from the FBI and a Black woman, who also wore a flight suit.

Jason said, "We've gotten clearance for you to take up the helicopter, Brett. Farrah is here to help with pre-flight."

Before Jason could say anything more, Brett said, "Eva's offered to come, and I think she should be on-board. Who knows what we'll find out there—what else might happen. That means we need someone with medical expertise. I can only take two more with me." He paused. Eva supposed the silence was to let the information sink in. "I'll let you all decide who gets the other seats. Farrah, let's get preflight done."

The trio of men circled into a tight knot. Eva assumed they were discussing who should go into the air and why.

Within minutes, the rotors started to spin.

Isaac and Ryan stepped away from Jason. "Looks like we're ready to go," said Isaac.

Eva ducked to avoid the downdraft as she slipped through the helicopter's open door. Brett was in the pilot's seat. Ryan sat next to him. Isaac was in the back seat. She settled into the empty seat and slipped on a headset.

"Buckle up," said Brett, his voice coming through the earphones.

She set the med kit on the floor, slid her arms into the five-point harness and gave Brett a thumbs-up. He turned toward the instrument panel and pushed the throttle forward. The helicopter rose from the ground. Soon, they were flying over Encantador.

At the edge of town, Eva found her grandmother's

neighborhood and then her house. It didn't matter that she was a grown woman. There was something magical about seeing the familiar from the air. She wanted to say, *Everything down there is so small. All the houses and cars look like toys*, but kept the cliché to herself. Instead, she asked, "How do you know where to go?"

Ryan turned in his seat. "A call was made to an associate of Decker's. Since it originated in this area, it's just a hunch that he was the one who made it." He retrieved a tablet from the floorboard. "We have some satellite images of the area."

He showed her the screen, a picture of dirt, scrub brush and a small white house with a car parked next to the door. The resolution was good—almost the same as what she saw out the window.

"The place you work." She paused, not able to recall the name.

"Texas Law," Isaac offered.

Oh yeah, that was it. "How did Texas Law get that kind of picture? I mean, do you all control a satellite?"

Isaac chuckled. "We don't have anything that fancy. Hell, we don't even have our own helicopter—that's why we're hitching a ride."

"Maybe that should be the agency's next purchase," said Ryan.

"It's something to consider," said Isaac.

Eva wasn't going to be ignored that easily. She said, "But you do have that photograph."

"It's courtesy of the NSA via the FBI," said Isaac. "We work with other agencies on many of our cases.

And finding and arresting Decker Newcombe is priority number one for a lot of them."

"One of the women he killed—the one whose murder was posted on the internet—lived next door to my grandmother." Eva wasn't sure why she shared that bit of information, but it seemed important.

"Is your grandma Gladys Tamke?" Ryan asked.

"She is."

"I know your grandmother then." Ryan powered down the tablet. "How's she doing?"

"Actually, she fell and is in the hospital."

"Tell me if she needs anything. I've done a few things around her house. My girlfriend, Kathryn Glass, lives across the street."

Baba had spoken about the handsome man who fixed her toilet and hung draperies. It must've been Ryan who'd helped all those times. It really was a small world, although she kept that cliché to herself, as well. So Ryan was the one who'd saved Kathryn's daughter from being killed during a live stream. It also meant he was the one who'd saved Decker from a burning building. "How's Kathryn's daughter? What's her name? Madison?"

"Morgan," said Ryan. "Physically, she recovered."

"Emotionally?" Eva asked.

Ryan shrugged. "She still has nightmares and refuses to be alone. She won't like that he's at large. I don't like it, either. She's been talking to a therapist, but it hasn't been long. Hopefully, she'll learn how to cope with what happened."

Brett said, "We'll be landing in one minute. There's

no way to hide a helicopter out here, so whoever's in that house knows we're coming. Be ready for anything."

Eva's pulse climbed. Had she really volunteered to go looking for Decker Newcombe? Honestly, she shouldn't be here.

Then again, it was too late to change her mind.

During his time in the army, Brett had flown into and out of several active combat zones. Each time he felt much the same as he did now. Anxiety clawed at his gut—and yet, he was hyperfocused. His hearing was sharper. His vision was clearer. He was ready to act in an instant.

The skids touched the ground, and just like troops trained to storm a beachhead, Isaac and Ryan exited the aircraft. They ran toward the small white house with their weapons drawn.

Eva stayed in the back seat of the chopper.

Over the past few days, she had become the most important person in the world to him. It wasn't just because she was the lone survivor from his crew. His feelings for her were wholly personal.

It took only minutes for Isaac and Ryan to enter and reemerge from the house. He could tell by the slump of their shoulders that they hadn't found what they were looking for. Ryan waved, and Brett powered down the engine. The rotors stopped spinning. He stripped off his headset and turned in his seat to look at Eva. The sun shone on her dark brown hair, bringing out the caramel color in some of her locks. Her skin was golden. She was so beautiful that his chest ached.

"We better go see what they want," she said.

"I guess so."

Brett opened the door and rounded the front of the helicopter. Together, they walked the short distance to where the security operatives waited.

"What's up?" Brett asked.

"There's a body inside," said Ryan. "Months ago, Decker mentioned that an older woman had been helping him live off the grid. The person inside looks to be older and female. It'd make sense that he came here. I can only guess why she ended up dead."

"Are you sure she's dead?" Eva asked.

"Positive," said Ryan. "There's a lot of blood around the body and no pulse."

Isaac picked up where Ryan left off. "We'll need to call this in and get crime-scene investigators here from both Mexico and the US. But for now, we need you to get back into the air and see if you can spot Decker."

Eva said, "I need to make sure she's actually deceased."

Brett assumed that her need to check was part of the oath she took as a nurse. Together, they walked into the small house.

The stench of meat left too long in the sun hung in the air. He swallowed down his rising nausea.

Like Ryan and Isaac had reported, a woman with her long gray hair in a braid lay on the floor. The front of her thin cotton dress was stained red. A pool of blood surrounded her body, making her look as if she floated on a lake of tar.

Eva donned a pair of surgical gloves before kneeling

next to the body. She touched the woman's wrist, feeling for a pulse. With a shake of her head, she pronounced, "Blood loss, I'd say. Until someone gets a good look at her, my guess is that it's from the gunshot." She pointed to a blackened hole in the middle of the woman's chest.

He hadn't noticed the discolored or torn cloth because of all the blood. "I can use the helicopter's radio to call this in."

"Before you do that—" Isaac inclined his chin, nodding to the woman on the ground "—I have a few questions. How long do you think she's been gone?"

"Not long." Eva stood. "It's hot in here, which means rigor mortis will set in quicker. It hasn't started yet. So, she's been dead less than a few hours."

"Which means," said Ryan, "Decker hasn't gotten too far."

Brett knew that the helicopter was the best way to search. He also knew that in the satellite photo, a white sedan had been parked in front of the house. "I can look for that car," he said.

Ryan nodded. "Thanks, man. We need to stay here and look for clues as to where Decker might be headed next."

Already, Brett's blood buzzed with the need to be airborne. "Eva, are you coming with me?"

She looked at him and back to the body. "Maybe I should stay here," she said, "with her."

"There's nothing you can do for the woman now," said Isaac. "But you can help with the aerial search."

"All right, then," she said, walking toward the door. She handed the med kit to Ryan. "You might need this."

"I hope not," he said, tucking the plastic box under his arm. "But thank you."

Without speaking, Eva and Brett walked toward the aircraft. The shadow of the rotors stretched along the ground. He stopped.

Eva took a few more steps before looking over her shoulder. "Everything okay?" she asked.

Brett knew that the chapter of his life that he'd shared with Eva was close to the end. But he didn't want their story to be over. "I just want you to know..." he began.

His words trailed off. Maybe he was wasting his time by saying anything. After all, she had a life of her own. She'd also been clear that there wasn't space in her life for a relationship. But so much had happened since she sent him that text.

"You just want me to know what?" she coaxed.

If he was going to say something to her, this was his last shot. "I don't know what's going to happen next in either of our lives. But I do know that whatever it is, in the past few days—although, it seems like it's been a year—you've become the reason I've kept going on. I can't lose you now that I've found you. I just want to give us a chance to be, well, *us*." He paused. "The thing is, I've fallen in love with you."

"Brett," she said, smiling, her eyes shining. "Stop talking and kiss me."

Those were the best words he'd ever heard. Brett didn't have a crystal ball. He couldn't read the future. But really, he didn't need to be. He knew that their perfect first date was just the beginning of their happily ever after.

He didn't expect the flight plan of life to clear. He expected storms and turbulence. The thing was, he didn't want to take the trip with anyone but Eva.

It took Brett only a few minutes to start the engine and get the helicopter into the air once more. As Brett lifted off the ground, Eva sat at his side.

For a single moment, in the air with the woman he loved, life was perfect.

Epilogue

One week later

Eva sat on the sofa in the living room of her grand-mother's house. Her ankle, still swollen and sore, was propped up on an ottoman with a pillow underneath. Two days earlier, she'd returned to SAMC and had been given an MRI. She had an appointment in a week to get the re-sults. Until then, she'd been ordered to stay off her foot.

When she was at San Antonio, Eva spoke to Darla and put in her notice. She'd also told her landlord that she was moving out at the end of the month. Within weeks, the ties that connected her to her old life would be cut, and she'd be starting over.

From the kitchen came the sounds of banging pans and the salty scent of bacon frying.

"Are you sure I can't help with anything, Baba?" Eva had to yell to be heard over the din of cooking.

Her grandmother appeared at the doorway, spatula in hand. "You just rest." She flicked the spatula like a conductor with a baton. "I'll take care of everything."

"I'm supposed to be taking care of you. Remember?"

"Having you here is taking care of me and my soul."

Eva had mixed feelings about being waited on. First, she loved that her grandmother cared. Truly, having someone around seemed to lift Baba's spirits. On the other hand, Eva hated to feel helpless. Beyond that, she was bored with just sitting. Honestly, how many word searches could one person do in a week?

"I need to get back to breakfast. We're having company."

"Company?" Eva echoed. "Who's coming over?" Although, she really didn't have to ask. She could guess. "Is Brett coming over again?"

"Since he's doing the grocery shopping, I thought that making him breakfast was a nice gesture."

"You don't have to keep inviting him over just for my sake."

"I'm not doing any of this for you. It's all for me. Who wouldn't want a handsome pilot around?" Her grandmother winked to show that she was teasing before disappearing once more into the kitchen.

Truth be told, Eva liked having Brett visit often. He'd helped her with more than one word search. He'd taken her out in his truck, just so she could get out of the house. In the moments when the terror of the crash returned, he held her and told Eva that she was safe.

Since the day they were rescued, Brett had spent most of his time in Encantador. He'd taken a leave of absence from San Antonio Medical Center. For now, he was staying in a spare room of Ryan's apartment. It wasn't like Brett was in the way; Ryan spent most of his time with his girlfriend, the local undersheriff, Kathryn Glass. Who also happened to live across the street from Baba.

The sound of a car door slamming came from the street. Instinctively, she flinched. So far, Decker Newcombe was still at large. There was no reason to think that he'd return to Encantador or even Mercy, much less look for her specifically. But until he was in jail, she'd always be jumpy.

She pulled a curtain aside. Brett's truck was parked next to the curb. He carried a tinfoil and plastic to-go container and was already striding up the walk.

He saw her peering out of the window and gave her a short wave. She smiled and relaxed, letting the curtain fall closed. Reaching for her crutches, she rose from the sofa and hobbled to the front door.

Brett stood on the threshold, his hand lifted and ready to knock.

"You're up early," she said.

"And you're up period. Aren't you supposed to be resting?"

"I'm not putting any weight on my foot," she said, lifting her injured leg to prove her point. "What's in the dish?"

Brett lifted the lid. Fragrant steam, both sweet and yeasty, escaped. "I made pancakes." He lifted a flapjack out of the tin, perfectly round and golden brown. "You want to try one?"

She took a bite. It was light, fluffy and sweet. "You're right," she said. "Best pancake ever."

"It's perfect, right?"

"Better than perfect," she said, although she wasn't exactly talking about the food.

Across the street, Ryan emerged from Kathryn's

house. He lifted his hand in greeting. "Hey, man," he called out to Brett. "I was just heading over to the apartment to chat with you. You got a minute?"

"Sure thing," said Brett. "What's up?"

Ryan jogged across the road and stopped at the end of the driveway. "This past week, Isaac and I figured something out. We can't find Decker using the resources we have right now. We bought an MD 600N. Or should I say that Texas Law purchased the helicopter. It's used, but in perfect shape. What we don't have is a pilot. That's where you come in." Ryan paused. "Basically, we want you on the team."

She watched Brett, trying to gauge his reaction. The thing was, if he lived in Encantador, they could be together daily. Was he really willing to make such a big change?

Brett exhaled. "Can I have a day or two to think it over?"

"I'll have Isaac call you," Ryan said. "He can tell you everything about the job. Expectations. Salary. Benefits. I do know that you'd be stationed here."

"Thanks," Brett said, "it means a lot to me. Once I talk to Isaac, I'll let him know."

"Texas Law was a lifeline for me," said Ryan. "It could be the same for you." He gave a final wave and crossed to the other side of the street.

Once he was gone, Eva released a breath she didn't recall holding. "So?" she prompted, taking the last bite of the pancake. "What do you think?"

"I'll have to see the actual offer," he said. "But I'm curious about your thoughts."

She swallowed. "I want what's best for you."

He reached for her and took her hand in his. "But what's best for us?"

"Obviously, if you moved here, we would see each other every day."

"Is that what you want?"

Having Brett nearby would mean tearing down the wall Eva had built around her heart long ago. Sure, she'd created the barrier to keep her safe. But it had also kept her alone. Pulling him closer, she said, "I want you. I want us. I want to see what kind of future we can create together."

"Done," he said, placing his lips on hers.

As she melted into the embrace, Eva didn't know what the future held. But with Brett at her side, they could face anything.

* * * * *

Look for Ana's story,
the next installment in
Jennifer D. Bokal's miniseries Texas Law
Coming soon to Harlequin Romantic Suspense!

HARLEQUIN
Reader Service

Enjoyed your book?

Try the perfect subscription for Romance readers and get more great books like this delivered right to your door.

See why over 10+ million readers have tried Harlequin Reader Service.

Start with a Free Welcome Collection with free books and a gift—valued over $20.

Choose any series in print or ebook.
See website for details and order today:

TryReaderService.com/subscriptions